He took her chin in one powerful hand and wrenched her face up towards his.

She didn't have time to voice the protest that formed in her mind. Her mouth was still opening to speak as his came down, hard and determined.

As a kiss, it was cruel and passionless, but as an act of punishment for rejecting him it was perfect. There was nothing of affection or warmth in it, only a cold-blooded determination to show her who was in control here.

But it didn't stay that way.

Because something happened in the moment that their lips touched. Something that charged the atmosphere, changed the truth of that kiss into something very new and very different.

From something meant to control and be controlled, in the space of a heartbeat it flared into something totally *out* of control.

Kate Walker was born in Nottinghamshire, but as she grew up in Yorkshire she has always felt that her roots are there. She met her husband at university, and originally worked as a children's librarian, but after the birth of her son she returned to her old childhood love of writing. When she's not working, she divides her time between her family, their three cats, and her interests in embroidery, antiques, film and theatre and, of course, reading.

Recent titles by the same author:

The Alcolar Family trilogy:

THE TWELVE-MONTH MISTRESS
THE SPANIARD'S INCONVENIENT WIFE
BOUND BY BLACKMAIL

THE ANTONAKOS MARRIAGE

BY
KATE WALKER

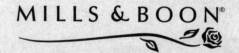

All the characters in this book have no existence outside the imagination of the author, and have no relation whatsoever to anyone bearing the same name or names. They are not even distantly inspired by any individual known or unknown to the author, and all the incidents are pure invention.

All Rights Reserved including the right of reproduction in whole or in part in any form. This edition is published by arrangement with Harlequin Enterprises II B.V. The text of this publication or any part thereof may not be reproduced or transmitted in any form or by any means, electronic or mechanical, including photocopying, recording, storage in an information retrieval system, or otherwise, without the written permission of the publisher.

This book is sold subject to the condition that it shall not, by way of trade or otherwise, be lent, resold, hired out or otherwise circulated without the prior consent of the publisher in any form of binding or cover other than that in which it is published and without a similar condition including this condition being imposed on the subsequent purchaser.

MILLS & BOON and MILLS & BOON with the Rose Device are registered trademarks of the publisher.

First published in Great Britain 2005.
Harlequin Mills & Boon Limited,
Eton House, 18-24 Paradise Road, Richmond, Surrey TW9 1SR

© Kate Walker 2005

ISBN 0 263 84204 5

Set in Times Roman 10½ on 11½ pt.
01-1205-53797

Printed and bound in Spain
by Litografia Rosés, S.A., Barcelona

CHAPTER ONE

THEO ANTONAKOS was not in the least impressed to learn that he was about to get a new stepmother.

He had never come to terms with his father's reputation with women. He'd lost count of the number of lovers who had drifted through the older man's life since his own mother's death and become, for a time, surrogate *materas* to him while he was growing up. Not one of them had stayed, though three of them had become Cyril's wife for a while, usually a very brief time.

Now it seemed that the fifth Mrs Antonakos was about to make her appearance. Quite frankly, Theo didn't hold out much expectation that she would last any longer than any of her predecessors, but she was indirectly responsible for the restlessness and the unsettled mood that were eating at him tonight.

He reached for his glass of wine and drained the rich red liquid from the bottom of it, slamming the glass back down on the table top with a crash that revealed the turmoil of his inner feelings.

He usually loved London's bustling vibrancy, the sense of people going places, living busy lives. The crowded streets, the lights, the hum of cars, reminded him of his home in Athens, the city life he had there, the cut and thrust of the business world that made every day a challenge he enjoyed.

But when it was dark and damp and *cold* as it was now on this October evening, then he wished he were anywhere but here. He missed the heat of the Greek sun on his back, the lazy lap of the ocean against the rocks of the island his family owned. He missed the sound of his native language. He missed his family. Hell, he missed *home*.

It had started with the letter that had arrived that morning.

One look at the stamp with the familiar Greek script had jarred him awake with a speed and roughness that had made his head spin. He hadn't even needed to check the postmark, or the rough, almost illegible scrawl of the address. He had known immediately just who it was from.

His father had broken his long silence and had written at last.

'Oh, come on, Red, lighten up. Sit down and have a drink with us!'

The rough-edged, slightly slurred comment followed by a chorus of laughter drifted over to him from across the other side of the bar, making him glance in that direction. A couple of youths were lounging around a table, beer bottles littering the polished surface.

But it was the woman with them who caught his attention. Caught and held it.

He couldn't see her face because she had her back to him. But what he could see was stunning. Physically, sexually stunning in a way that made desire twist, sharp and hot, in his gut in immediate reaction.

Long hair in a glorious, burnished red gold cascaded down the slender length of her back, gleaming with coppery highlights even under the shaded lamps of the bar. She was tall and shapely: narrow shoulders, neat hips, a pert, tight bottom under the clinging skirt of her black dress.

Skirt? His faint laugh denied the description. That wasn't a skirt, it was a pelmet—little more than an extended belt, leaving exposed the slim, elegant length of her legs in sheerest black nylon, right down to the point where her feet were pushed into the polished, ridiculously high-heeled shoes.

'Anything you like, sweetheart...'

There was something about her that compelled him to watch her.

And he had been without a woman too long. That was the real reason he was interested. Ever since Eva had walked out three months ago, there had been no female company in his life.

He could have had plenty—he knew without false modesty that his dark looks attracted female attention and interest. Add to that the appeal of the wealth that came from both his family background and the results of his own efforts, and he rarely had to spend a night alone unless he wanted to.

But lately that knowledge hadn't satisfied him. He was edgy, wanted more.

Not with Eva, though. That was why they'd argued and why she'd walked. Eva had thought that she was onto a good thing. She had had wedding bells and gold rings in her dreams, and he had had to disillusion her about that pretty forcefully. As a result, she'd left. Eva wasn't the kind of girl to stay around when she knew she wasn't going to get what she wanted.

And if he was honest with himself, he really hadn't missed her.

'No, really, no thanks.'

Her voice fell into one of those sudden lapses into silence in which even the quietest voice sounded clear and audible in the stillness of the room.

And what a voice! It was low and sensual, surprisingly husky for a woman. It made him imagine hearing that voice whispering to him in the deep, warm darkness of a king-size bed. His mouth dried, his body tightened just to think of it. But the next moment, the sexy mood vanished, the erotic thoughts driven away by a dramatic change in her tone.

'I said *no, thank you.*'

Theo was on his feet before he was even aware of having reacted. There had been an edge to her words, a note of unease, of total rejection of the position in which she found herself. She wasn't happy, it was obvious.

Half a dozen long, forceful strides took him across the room to come up close behind her. Neither she nor the men she was talking to had even noticed him.

Skye Marston knew that she was in trouble.

In fact, she had known it from three heartbeats into the conversation she had foolishly started with these two. She should never have stopped, never responded to their casually friendly greeting on her way into the room.

Their *apparently* casually friendly greeting.

She had come into the bar on a whim. It had looked crowded, brightly lit and warm, in contrast to the cold wind and driving rain of the street outside. And she had wanted desperately to be with people. She had spent too much time on her own, and being on her own left her vulnerable to her unhappy thoughts.

Was it really less than a month since her father had broken down and admitted that his money problems were far worse than he had let on? That in an attempt to deal with them, he had made a real mess of things by 'borrowing' from his boss, Greek millionaire Cyril Antonakos, the owner of the hotels he managed—and, even worse, he had now been found out. He faced a lengthy prison sentence if charges were pressed.

'I can't go to jail, Skye!' he had wept. 'Not now, not with your mother so ill! It would kill her. She just can't manage without me. You have to help me!'

'I'll do anything I can, Dad.' Skye had reacted instinctively, knowing there was nothing else she could say.

Her mother's heart condition had been a cause of great

concern for some time, but lately her condition had deteriorated. Now it seemed that if the next operation she had didn't succeed, her only hope was a transplant. 'Anything at all—though I don't know what help I can be!'

But her father had known. Cyril Antonakos had already proposed a way out of the terrible trap in which Andrew Marston found himself. And Skye had listened in horror as he had revealed just how vital she was to their scheme. Cyril wanted an heir. To achieve that end, obviously he needed a wife and, as his last marriage had ended in an acrimonious divorce, he had selected Skye as the potential mother of his child. If she married him, gave him the heir he craved, he wouldn't prosecute.

In order to save Andrew Marston from imprisonment, she was being asked to marry a man older than her father.

And tomorrow she had to give him her answer.

That was why she was here tonight. That was why she was out on her own, spending her one last night of freedom in the impersonal bright lights and busy streets of London. She could only pray that those bright lights—and the crowded bars—were enough to distract her from what tomorrow would bring.

Not giving herself time to reconsider, she had swung into the wide doorway, struggling with the big glass doors, pushing her way through the crowd, trying to reach the bar.

And immediately she had felt that she had made a mistake.

The bar was warm and bright, true. It was also very busy. And everyone there seemed to know someone else. No one was on their own, without anyone else to talk to, to smile at.

And even if they had been alone, she told herself, no one else could ever be quite so lonely, quite so isolated as she felt right now.

She had been about to turn round and go back out when

she had spotted the one other person who, like her, was on his own.

Should she—*could* she—make herself go up and talk to him? That had been her plan from the start. To meet someone and talk to them, so, hopefully, driving away this appalling sense of isolation and loss, melting the cruel block of ice that seemed to surround her world, and giving her some moments of freedom and relaxation before the world closed in on her again.

But this man didn't look the type who could fulfil that hope for her. He was too big, too dark, too dangerous-looking. His long body lounged in the chair, apparently at ease, but there was an air of menace, of carefully leashed power, about him that made her heart kick inside her chest, so that she caught her breath in shock. His black-haired head was turned away from her, and hooded eyes stared down into a glass half-filled with red wine.

It was almost as if she had come across a sleek, honed hunting cat crouching in wait in some small, shaded jungle clearing. Just seeing him slowed her steps to a halt, making her hesitate and rethink.

And that was when the call from the nearest table had distracted her.

'Hello, darling. Looking for someone?'

If she hadn't been so diverted by the appearance of the dark-haired man in the corner, so desperate for company and distraction, Skye would have simply switched on an automatic smile, murmured something about having 'just spotted them, thank you,' and moved on. But her steps had already slowed, she had stopped beside the table, and somehow she couldn't find the words to extricate herself.

And they clearly thought that she was with them for the evening—and more. Their smiles, the hot, lascivious way their eyes travelled over her, made her feel uneasy. She might have been looking for a last chance to spend her time as a free, single twenty-two-year-old, but this was not what she'd had in mind.

She tried to turn down the offers of a drink with what she hoped was an apologetic smile, an expression of regret, but she could see that they weren't appeased. The blond was growing noticeably aggressive, and when she tried to step back and move away she found that his black-haired friend had grabbed her arm and was gripping it in a bruisingly tight hold.

'So what's wrong—aren't we good enough for you?'

'No—really—I—I'm waiting for someone.'

'Like who?' Frank disbelief sounded roughly in his voice.

'My—my boyfriend. He said—he'd meet me here.'

The blond made an elaborate play of looking around the room, searching for the imaginary boyfriend.

'Then I think you've been stood up, Red. He's clearly not coming for you.'

The grip on her arm tightened cruelly, pulling her closer so that she had to bend slightly to adjust to the tug on her wrist.

'He—he's just late.'

'Do you know what I think, Red?'

It was a mocking whisper, a malicious gleam lighting in his eyes.

'I think he's not coming. In fact, I have this suspicion that you're telling me lies—that this lover of yours just doesn't exist.'

'Oh, but he does.'

Skye jumped like a startled cat as the words came from behind her. The deep, gorgeously accented, sexy *male* voice was the last thing she had ever anticipated. It was the fantasy she might have wished for—the dream lover turning up to rescue her from the awkward, uncomfortable situation in which she found herself.

But this was no fantasy. The startled gaze of her tormentors had gone from her face to somewhere behind the back of her head, shock and consternation showing in their eyes. The controlling grip on her wrist had loosened, letting her pull free.

'Oh!'

The soft cry of shock was pushed from her as a pair of tightly muscled arms slid round her waist from behind. A hard, powerful frame was pressed up against her back, its heat and strength reaching right through the material of her jacket, to her skin, her bones—seeming to scorch her soul.

She felt safe, protected, *surrounded* by this unknown man. His warmth and strength enclosed her, the sound of his breathing tantalised her ears, and the scent of his skin filled her nostrils.

'Sorry I'm late, darling,' the husky voice murmured against her neck. 'You know how these meetings drag on. But I'm here now.'

'Mmm.'

It was all she could manage and she didn't care if it sounded more like a sigh of sensual response than any coherent answer.

Her body was tingling all over, burning in instant response to just this unknown man's touch. She couldn't see his face—the only parts of his body that were visible to her were the hands that were clasped around her waist.

And they were intensely *masculine* hands. Big and square and capable-looking. They dwarfed her own smaller, slimmer fingers as they closed warmly over them. No rings. The only adornment was a sleek platinum watch on one wrist, just above an immaculate white shirt cuff, the steel-grey of an elegant and expensive jacket.

'Forgive me?'

'Oh, yes!'

How could she say anything else? She would have

agreed to anything, accepted anything from him. It was impossible to think straight, and what tiny fragments of thoughts still lingered inside her head were totally shattered, blasted into oblivion by what he did next.

She sensed movement behind her, just out of sight. Felt the brush of silky hair against her cheek, then suddenly there was the press of warm lips against the back of her neck. Her breath caught in her throat; her heart thudded hard against her ribcage, and her head went back against a strong, supportive shoulder, her eyes half closing in sensual response.

'Hey!'

The stranger's voice was soft, faintly reproving, edged with a disturbing laughter.

'Not here, darling,' he went on wickedly. 'Better wait until we get home!'

Home! She wasn't going home with this man...

That brought her back to the present in the blink of an eyelid, her head coming up again sharply, her mouth opening on a gasp of protest. But the protest never had a chance to form because the man behind her spoke again before she had a chance to say a word.

'Time to go, sweetheart. Say goodbye to your friends.'

It was the way he said *friends* that alerted her. She had been in danger of giving away their pretence. If she had voiced her protest, she would have made it clear to the men at the table that her rescuer was not the lover she had claimed him as.

'Goodbye, guys! Th-thanks for keeping me company.'

Just who was this man who had come to her rescue so unexpectedly? The question raged in her mind as she made herself turn, ready to walk off with him, struggling to look as if this were something she did every day.

He slid his hand into hers, lacing his strong fingers with hers, holding her in a way that felt light and gentle, but which she was sure would be even harder to break away from than the dark-haired man's hold had been.

'Come on, let's get out of here.'

He was tall, and strongly built, that much she could tell from the swift, sidelong glances she slanted in his direction, not daring to actually turn and stare. In the shadowy light of the bar, his face was turned from her, eyes fixed on the doorway towards which his determined strides were taking them. She could only let herself be pulled along in his wake, wanting to be well away from her earlier tormentors before she did what she knew she was going to have to do and put the brakes on sharply, saying, 'This far and no further.'

'Hang on a minute...' she tried, but he either didn't hear or pretended not to. His ruthless path through the bar didn't falter, and where she had struggled through the crowds on her way in, now they just seemed to part smoothly to let him through.

The next moment they were at the door and moving down the steps into the street.

'Now hang on!'

She dug her heels in as she spoke, mentally slamming on the brakes and praying that his strength and power wouldn't just drag her over, tumbling ignominiously down the stone stairs after him.

'That's far enough!'

This time her voice reached him. Either that, or the pull on his hand was enough to drag him to a halt. He stopped abruptly, then whirled round, coming to face her, and she saw his features for the first time in the full glow of the light of the street lamps.

She'd seen them before. Seen that strong-boned, forcefully arrogant face. The jet-black, deep-set eyes above slashing cheekbones, the long, straight sweep of a nose, and the fall of rich, thick hair, darker than the night's shadows around him.

'You!'

The word escaped on a cry of shock as she recognised the man she had seen at the other side of the bar. The only other person who had been on his own in the busy, noisy room.

The man she had not dared to risk approaching because some intuitive sense of fear had held her back. Her instincts had sprung straight to red alert, flashing warning signs before her eyes and shrieking, 'Danger—keep away! Don't touch!' even before she had had a chance to think why. She just knew that something deep and primitive inside her had made her feel that he was someone to be treated with the intense caution with which she might approach a prowling jungle cat if she came face to face with it out hunting.

And seen up close he looked even more so. More dangerous; more devastating. More blatantly masculine. More shockingly attractive—and yet even his undeniable sexual appeal had a worrying core of threat at the bottom of it.

This wasn't the sort of man she usually encountered. He was nothing like the men she had known at home and in the office, the few, friendly dates she had ever been out on. He was beyond her experience, beyond her knowledge— and very definitely beyond her control.

Those instincts were working overtime again—and this time they were yelling at her that she was completely out of her depth with this man.

And if she wasn't very much mistaken, she had just jumped right out of the frying-pan and straight into the very heart of the fire.

CHAPTER TWO

'ME?'

THEO'S response to Skye's shocked exclamation was as calm and relaxed as he could make it, though any real control was the last thing he felt capable of.

He should never have touched her.

His body still burned at the thought of it; his brain had almost melted in the burn of the fierce, erotic heat that had flooded every inch of his body, making him hard and hungry in a second. He still ached from the sudden ebbing of the blazing tide, the effect of the cold night air that had hit him as soon as they had left the bar.

He should never have touched her, but what he hadn't anticipated was the way that she had responded to him.

He'd thought she felt it too.

If she hadn't, then what the hell had she meant by the way she'd reacted—resting her head against his shoulder, leaning back into him?

But now she was behaving as if she thought he was a demon from hell and not at all the person she'd been hoping for

'You were expecting someone else?'

'N-no—not exactly,' she stammered. 'I—it's just—I never thought that you'd be the one to come to my rescue. I should thank you,' she added, too belatedly to smooth his very ruffled feelings.

'Think nothing of it.'

A wave of his hand dismissed her stumbling thanks. Theo was well aware of the way that the frustrated demands of his aroused body were distorting his mood, making him

16

feel bad-tempered and edgy. And what made a bad mood infinitely worse was the way that, seeing her face full on now, in the light from the doorway, he found that the promise suggested by her back, her profile, indoors, was more than fulfilled by the reality.

She was *gorgeous.* A pale, oval face. Stunning light coloured eyes, with incredibly thick, lush lashes. A full, soft mouth seemed just made for kisses, and the thoughts that imagining that mouth on his own skin triggered off were so X-rated that he was glad of the shadows in the street, the darkness of the evening, that hid his response from her.

'And I should introduce myself.'

Her hand came out, stiffly formal.

'I'm—Skye…'

The hesitation before her name and the way that she didn't add a surname told him she didn't want to trust him with the full details of her identity. Fair enough, that was fine with him.

'Anton,' he growled, knowing he was forced to take her hand, but making the contact as brief and brusque as possible before letting it drop.

He didn't want a repeat of the cruelly demanding sensations he'd experienced before, especially when it seemed that this Skye was determined to be on her way as soon as possible and there was no chance of taking things any further.

'Anton.'

The way that she echoed the name he had given her made him wonder if she really knew, or suspected, it was not genuine.

He didn't give a damn one way or another. Even here, in England, the Antonakos name—and, more importantly, the Antonakos fortune—was so well known that the realisation he was a member of that family was enough to create an interest where there wasn't one, to put a speculative light in the eye of anyone he met.

And, in his experience, women were the worst offenders. Along with the name Antonakos, they saw the prospect of a meal ticket for life; a future of luxury and ease, if they could just play their cards right.

As he was not at all sure what sort of cards this Skye, whoever she was, was about to play; he preferred to keep his own—and the truth of his identity—very close to his chest.

Not that she seemed in the least interested right now. Those pale eyes were scanning the street, looking up and down the road.

'Are you looking for someone?'

Suspicion made him voice it. Damn it, had he got this all wrong from the start? He cursed under his breath at the way that thought made him feel. He didn't want her to have been really waiting for anyone. He had assumed that the lover she had claimed was imaginary—had *wanted* him not to exist.

The truth was that he wanted this woman for himself, and right now he was prepared to do whatever it took to get her.

'Was that boyfriend you mentioned real after all?'

'Oh, no.'

The shake of her head sent the red-gold fall of her hair flying around her face, tiny drops of rain shimmering in its depths from the drizzle that was falling.

'No, I made him up in the hope they would let me go. I wasn't looking for anyone—just a taxi.'

'I can give you a lift anywhere you want to go.'

'A taxi will be fine.' It was the vocal equivalent of several steps backwards and away from him. No physical action could have put more of a distance between them.

A black cab was approaching and she lifted a hand to

hail it, but too late. It swept past in a spray of water from the puddles filling the gutter, spattering her skirt and legs with mud.

'I can give you a lift anywhere you want to go.'

The way he repeated his exact words of just moments before brought Skye's eyes to his face in a rush. Meeting the glittering darkness of his gaze, seeing the way that the muscles of his jaw were drawn tight, she knew a sinking sense of realisation.

She'd insulted him with her refusal. He was angry too, something that told her how much her rejection had meant to him.

'I—was trying to be sensible,' she managed.

'Isn't it a little late for that now?'

'What do you mean by that?'

'Well, the situation you got yourself into back there—' His dark head nodded towards the noisy, smoky bar. 'That was hardly the action of a *sensible* person.'

The deliberate emphasis on the repeated word goaded her, as she was sure it was meant to do, sparking her temper and bringing her chin up, eyes flashing angry fire.

'I didn't exactly *ask* for that!' she snapped. 'It just happened!'

'I only offered you a lift in my car.'

The resignation in his tone had a hard edge to it, one that warned her of the way his temper was fraying at the edges.

'I'm sor—' she began, but he ignored her and rushed on angrily.

'I was brought up never to let a woman risk being on her own, if I could do anything to help her.'

'Then get me a taxi—please.'

She prayed he wouldn't argue further. She was rapidly losing her grip on her self-control as it was.

'No.'

It was cold and hard and unyielding, and it chilled her blood just to hear it.

Out of the frying-pan and into the fire. The ominous phrase that had slipped into her head in the first moments they had been outside now pounded round and round inside her skull until she felt as if her mind would explode.

'You don't need a taxi. I will take you wherever you want to go.'

Skye's eyes closed on a shudder of horror as she tried to imagine just how that scenario would play out. She didn't even want to think of her father's reaction if she was to arrive home in a strange car—with an unknown man. Even less did she want to imagine the way her prospective fiancé would view that situation.

Oh, why had she ever thought she could do this? Why had she let herself believe that she could fling herself into one night of liberty just to try and put a temporary barrier between herself and the future that lay ahead of her?

Why had she ever imagined that she could have one night in which she lived the same sort of life as her friends, as other young women her age? One night of total freedom, of irresponsibility, of reckless abandon before the walls of restraint and restriction closed round her once and for all?

She had never been able to live that way even when she had had her freedom—the freedom of youth. So why had she ever thought she could do it now, just for tonight? She had been out of her depth from the start—and she was sinking in deeper with every second that passed.

'I'll get one myself, then.'

She swung away from him violently, knowing in her heart that she was really running from herself, not from him. But she was closer to the edge of the pavement than she thought. Her heel caught on the kerb, twisted awkwardly and went from beneath her. She would have gone flying off the footpath, falling headlong onto the wet tarmac, into the middle of the road and the path of the on-coming cars, if the man beside her hadn't reacted with in-stinctive speed.

'Skye—look out!'

In the blink of an eye he was beside her, reaching out and catching her before her stumble became a fall. She was held tight, hauled up into arms that felt like tempered steel as they tensed, took her weight and then pulled her back to safety.

Safety? Or right back into the heart of danger?

Skye had no way of knowing and her head was whirling too much in the aftermath of the shock of her near fall to be able to think clearly.

The position she was in didn't help either. Anton had spun her round as he caught her up so that now she was clamped tight against him, enfolded in his arms, with her body crushed against the hard length of his, her head on his chest, her cheek above the heavy, heated thud of his heart, the sound of his pulse in her ears.

And it was all happening again.

Just as it had when he had come up behind her in the bar, so now her blood was heating in urgent response to his closeness, her heart racing in time with the fierce beat of his. She was surrounded by him, held in the heat and hardness of his grip, the clean, male scent of his body sur-rounding her, melting her thoughts inside her head.

It felt like coming home.

It felt as if she had always been there. As if this was truly where she belonged. Where she most wanted to be in all the world. And with the instinctive cuddling movement of a small creature seeking comfort from the cold, hard world outside, she snuggled closer, burying her face in his shirt front, her hands sliding under his jacket, her arms going round the narrow waist.

She felt his grip tighten even more, and his dark head

bent, his face coming so close to hers that the faint roughness of the beginnings of evening growth of beard rubbed
lightly against the delicate skin of her cheek. She sensed—
unbelievingly—the warm caress of his mouth on her neck,
at the base of her ear, and heard his deep sigh as he whispered harshly against the delicate lobe.

'Skye, don't go—stay! I want you to stay.'

'What?'

Had he really said what she thought she had heard? She
couldn't believe it. It couldn't be true. It had to be her ears
deceiving her or the voice of her own hungry longings
sounding inside her head, telling her what she most wanted
to hear.

But she couldn't have heard it. Men like this Anton
didn't suddenly beg girls like her to stay with them, not on
such brief acquaintance.

Had he really said…?

Tilting her head, she tried to look up into his face, to
read the answer there, but even as she moved his dark head
came down towards hers. His mouth closed over hers and
captured it in a searing, blazing kiss that sent a sensation
like a lightning bolt fizzing through her body, right down
to the tips of her toes.

This couldn't be happening, was the one brief thought
that Skye managed before her brain short-circuited and
thinking became impossible. Before it was replaced only
by feeling.

His mouth was pure enticement, pure sinful seduction.
His kiss worked a spell on her that had her melting against
him, into him, losing herself in the feeling of becoming
part of him. Her lips parted, encouraging the heated inva-
sion of his tongue, her sighing moan a sound of pure surrender, all that was female in her responding to the darkly
elemental male in him. Something rich and dark and deeply

sensual uncoiled way down low in her body and set up a heavy, honeyed pounding between her thighs.

The sounds and the lights of the street became nothing but a blur in the back of her mind as the strength of his hold lifted her up onto her toes, almost off her feet. Powerful hands thrust into the fall of hair, sweeping it back from around her face as hard fingers dug into her skull. The rain came down harder, colder, but she was lost and oblivious to it, adrift in a heated world where nothing else could reach her.

In the distance someone wolf-whistled, and slowly, reluctantly, they drew apart, breath coming heavily, eyes wide, expressions slightly dazed as they met each other's gaze and acknowledged the primitive fires they had lit between them.

'I...' Skye began, but her voice broke in the middle, failing her completely as the reality of what had happened to her hit home like a savage blow to her head.

This was what it was all about. This was what male-female relationships really meant. What those words like *desire* and *passion* and *hunger* had had hidden behind them, unrecognised by her until now.

Now.

The single word sounded like a knell inside her head, deadening her thoughts and bringing the cruel sting of tears to her eyes.

Now, when it was too late. When a malevolent fate had stepped in and decided her future for her.

When she knew that these delights, this sort of happiness, were to be denied to her for ever. She had learned the truth too late, only to have it snatched away from her in the same moment that she discovered it. And with no chance of anything more.

Except for tonight, a tiny voice whispered in her mind, bringing with it dreams and hopes of the sort that she had never allowed into her thoughts before. Dreams that made her shiver just to contemplate them.

Dreams that were here, now, within her reach, and all she had to do was to stretch out a hand and grasp them, make them hers, for tonight; for one night only.

'Skye?' the man called Anton questioned softly, making her realise how long she had been standing there, silent, distant, locked in the shadowed, ominous darkness of her thoughts.

The heat of his body still enclosed her, His hold had loosened, but she still pressed up against the powerful length of his body, feeling the hard ridge against her stomach that spoke of the desire that had been in his kiss. The same desire that had been in hers. That still throbbed along every nerve pathway, pulsed in her blood.

He had wanted her every bit as she had wanted him—he still did.

But she had only met him tonight.

'I won't hurt you.' His voice was low and husky with need. So low and husky that it shocked her to think that she could ever have such an effect on any man—least of all *this* man. This tall, darkly imposing, devastating man.

'I promise you, you'll be safe with me. I swear...'

Her heart slammed against the wall of her ribcage, jerky and uneven, coming close to panic at just the thought of what she was considering. But the ache of need still suffused her own body and wouldn't let her go.

If only this had happened sooner. If only she had met this Anton before...

But no. That was to wish for the impossible. Her fate had been sealed and she had no alternative but to go down the path that had been chosen for her. The path she had agreed to.

The path she had had no choice but to agree to.

From tomorrow, everything would change. From tomorrow her life would no longer be her own.

Skye's teeth dug down hard into the softness of her bottom lip, scoring sharp little crescents into the delicate pink flesh.

Tomorrow.

Last week she had prayed that she could run away. She had dreamed of it, longed for it, hoped for a chance. But there was no chance. Too many people depended on her. If she had had any doubts about that, then the latest news only this week of how dangerous her mother's heart condition really was had destroyed them for ever. She couldn't run away and leave them all in the lurch.

But there was tonight.

Tonight she could run away—at least temporarily—from everything that was weighing her down. She could escape into a world of fantasy and sensual delight. A world that was so unreal she couldn't really believe it was happening to her. A world in which, for once in her life—for the one and only time—just for a few short hours, she could experience the full heights of passion and the fierce sensuality that she had tasted so briefly just a few moments before.

One of the hardest things to accept about this marriage to Cyril Antonakos was the fact that her unwanted wedding night would be her first experience of sex. She was still a virgin and had never known any man who could make her feel enough to want to change that situation.

Until now.

Now she couldn't bear the thought that a man nearing sixty would be her first, her only lover—when there was this man who only had to touch her and she felt as if she were going up in flames.

She could have tonight.

I promise you, you'll be safe with me. I swear...

He didn't even have to know her name. And tomorrow,

as in some modern-day Cinderella story, reality would close in around her once again.

But she would have had tonight.

If only she could bring herself to answer him. If only she could find the courage to say…

'Skye?'

Her name was rough on his tongue now, raw impatience and that devastating accent turning it into something new and strange. A sound she didn't recognise as the name she heard every day.

'Are you ever going to answer me?'

Skye tried. Swallowing hard to ease the dryness of her throat, she fought for the control, the strength she needed.

But then his long-fingered hand came under her chin, lifting it so that her face came up to meet his, her grey eyes meeting and locking with the deep, deep blackness of his. Drowning in their darkness.

He bent his head slowly and his mouth took hers. This time his kiss had none of the fierce, wild passion of moments before; instead it was soft and slow and heartbreakingly tender. It seemed to draw her soul out of her body, melt her bones, so that she was trembling against him, needing the potent strength of his body to support her so that she didn't fall to the ground.

'So tell me, my beauty,' he whispered in a voice that was as dark and rich as the black velvet night sky above them. 'Will you go or will you stay?'

My beauty, Skye thought hazily.

No one, not even her mother, had ever called her beautiful. Or made her feel it the way his kiss made her feel right now, here in this cold, rain-spattered street.

And suddenly there was only one answer to give him. Only one answer she *could* give him.

She had to have tonight. She might regret it in the morning, when reality hit her in the face. But the one thing she was sure of was that she could never regret it as much as she would bitterly regret saying no.

And so she lifted her head and kissed him back, putting her answer into the caress, but knowing she had to speak it too.

'Oh, yes,' she breathed softly, confidently. 'Yes, of course I'll stay. But on one condition…'

CHAPTER THREE

THEO flicked on the light and surveyed the room before him with a critical eye, frowning as he did so.

'Are you sure that this is what you want?'

He supposed that the room was all right, as hotel rooms went. It was at least clean and reasonably sized, with a comfortable-looking bed, and the usual furniture and fittings. Through a door off to one side was the tiny *en suite* bathroom, severely tiled in plain, cold white, with toiletries, towels and bath robes all in the same non-colour.

It was all totally soulless, functional but impersonal, and therefore unwelcoming. And not at all the sort of place he would have thought that he would end up in tonight.

But then, nothing tonight had gone the way he had expected it.

He had certainly never anticipated ending up in an anonymous hotel room with a woman who stirred every single one of his most primitive senses, but whose first name was the only thing he knew about her.

'We're strangers,' she had said, 'and I want to keep it that way. You don't know me and I don't know you—that's the way it has to be.'

No way! That was his first response. He actually stiffened, half turned to walk away, but she was still so close to him, he still had his arms around her, and the hot blood racing through his veins, the hungry need that clamoured at his senses, blurred his thoughts.

He couldn't let her go.

He had known that in the moment that he had seen her turn to hail a taxi to take her away and out of his life. And

28

if she went now, then she would be gone for ever. He would have no way of tracking her down. She would disappear into the night and he would never see her again; never know anything more about her.

'You ask a lot, lady,' he managed, his voice husky and rough.

She didn't show any sign of reconsidering. Her light-coloured gaze held his unwaveringly, and her soft mouth firmed to a determined line.

'It's that or nothing,' she said, reaching up a slim hand to smooth it across the front of his shirt, and the small movement brought a waft of her scent up to his nostrils, tantalising his senses and drying his mouth.

Beneath the caress of her fingers, his skin burned and his heart kicked savagely, making his pulse throb, his senses swim.

'That or nothing,' she repeated and he knew that he could never live with 'nothing'. He would always curse himself if he let this woman get away from him now.

'Whatever you want, lady,' he said, knowing it was nothing less than the truth. 'Whatever you want.'

And what she wanted was this.

For tonight at least.

Well, he would let her get away with it for tonight—after all, she wasn't the only one who had been a little...economical with the truth. But tomorrow always came.

Tomorrow he would be asking a lot of questions. And he'd want some very definite answers to all of them.

Meanwhile, he'd spend tonight convincing her that it wasn't 'that or nothing' at all.

'Skye?' he questioned now when the woman who had come into the room just behind him didn't answer. 'What is it? Have you changed your mind about tonight? Do you want to go back on this—renege on what we agreed?'

Did she?

Did she want to back out of the deal? Was that what she wanted?

They were the questions Skye had been asking herself ever since they'd come upstairs. No—before that. The truth was that her courage and conviction had been seeping away from the moment that she had agreed to stay with him.

It was obvious that she'd shocked him to the core with her blunt announcement that if she stayed then he must never ask her her full name, and never give her his.

She'd thought that he was going to walk away when she'd said that. Certainly his expression had seemed to promise that he was going to reject her outrageous proposition out of hand. His whole face had closed off, shutters seeming to come down behind the brilliant black eyes, until every one of his features had appeared to be carved in cold, unyielding marble.

But then he had blinked once, very slowly, and nodded his dark head.

'No,' she said now, miserably aware of the way that her own inner tension made her voice sound tight and hard, coldly distant. 'No, I'm not reneging on anything. It's just…'

Just that I'm no good at this.

The words were burning on her tongue, but she swallowed them back hastily, closing her eyes against the terrible anxiety she was feeling. She couldn't say them, not here, not now, not in this situation. Her stomach muscles were tying themselves into tight, painful knots, twisting each nerve harder and harder with every heartbeat.

'Just what?'

His voice sounded disturbingly close and when her eyes flew open again it was to find that he had taken several long strides forward. He was standing right in front of her, so near that if she just lifted her hand she could touch him without even stretching out her fingers.

And she wanted to touch him. The tips of her fingers tingled with the remembrance of the way his skin, his hair had felt to their touch. Her palms felt again the heat of the muscles beneath his shirt, sensed the thudding of his heart under the strong bones of his chest.

If she slicked her tongue along her lips, she could still taste him, clean, musky, intensely masculine, making her heart skip a beat. And she wanted that taste, those sensations all over again. She wanted to lose herself in that wonderful, sizzling feeling that flooded her senses, swamping her mind and leaving her incapable of thought, knowing only need.

She *wanted* this man.

'Just what?' he prompted again, more roughly this time.

I want you to hold me—to make me forget…

'Just that I wish you would kiss me again.'

'Oh, that!'

It was edged with laughter, threaded through with a knowing triumph.

'You only had to ask.'

He was already moving forward, taking her in his arms, drawing her close to him with the confidence of a man who was sure of his appeal; who had no doubt that he was wanted.

'So tell me, sweetheart…'

A caressing hand slid under her chin, lifting her face to his, and his glittering black eyes locked with her cloudy grey ones, holding her gaze, keeping her so still that even her heartbeat seemed to freeze.

'Where shall I kiss you? Here?'

The warm pressure of his mouth on her forehead was like a butterfly landing, light, delicate, there and gone again so swiftly that she barely even noticed it was there until she felt its loss. And when she did, her lips parted on a sigh of melancholy delight.

'Or here…?'

This time he caressed her cheek, dropping a kiss just below her temple, on the left and then again on the right, making her breathing deepen, her senses start to stir.

'Or perhaps here…?'

Softly, deliberately, he kissed her eyes shut, his lips lingering on the lids just long enough to seal them closed. At least, that was the way it felt to Skye, who found herself locked into a world of sensual darkness where every other sense seemed heightened and sharply sensitised to everything about him.

She could hear each breath he took, low and steady, matching the beat of his heart. His scent was on the air around her, that warm, clean, male essence, subtly blended with the tang of lime and spice in his cologne. When he took her hands in his, the heat seared across her skin like an electric current making her fingers curl in instant response, her breath catch sharply in her throat.

And it was all happening again.

She was melting inside, all the tension seeping out of her body so that she almost expected to see it pool on the floor at her feet. The honeyed pulse of desire was starting through her veins once more, sending the waves of yearning along the path of every nerve and setting them alight with need.

'That will do for a start,' she managed, amazed at her own boldness. A daring that was bolstered by the darkness behind her closed lids.

She couldn't see the man who held her, couldn't look into the darkness of his eyes and read anything—or nothing—from them. She could only *feel,* enclosed in her own private, secret world of sensations she had never known before, but now wanted to experience so much more.

She wanted to plunge into them like a swimmer diving straight into the deepest pool, letting the waters crash over her head and submerge her completely. Wanted to know it all. Wanted to snatch at things greedily and hungrily, grabbing them to her and swallowing them whole.

But Anton seemed determined to take things slowly. When she made a tiny movement of impatience he hushed her softly, smoothing the sound from her lips with a gentle finger.

'Not so fast, my lovely. We have all night.'

All night...

It had a wonderful sound. A sound that seemed to promise hours that would stretch out and out in a never-ending way, delivering pleasure for as long as she could stand it. But at the same time, Skye knew just how quickly those hours would fly by. How soon they would be over.

She had this one chance to know the sensuous delights that instinct told her were ahead of her. She couldn't waste them.

She *wouldn't* waste them. Already her body was on fire with anticipation and longing and she was trembling in his arms, grateful for the security of his hold that was all that kept her upright.

'Anton...'

His name was a moan of need on her lips and she felt as well as heard the soft laughter that shook his powerful frame.

'I know, sweetheart,' he told her and the new thickness in his voice revealed only too clearly just how much he did know. 'I know the way you're feeling—but, believe me, this will be worth taking slowly. It will be worth waiting for. Just go with me on this—let me show you...'

He was kissing her again now, his mouth taking a burning trail from her temple, down to her jaw before it captured her lips again. The touch of his mouth on her skin, the magic it could work, was threatening her ability to think. But there was one vital, practical matter she *had* to think of because the possible consequences if she didn't were too horrific even to consider.

She had just this one night; she couldn't risk the nightmare of any physical legacy that might result from it. That would destroy her and her family at a single stroke.

'Do you…?'

It was a struggle to get the words out and not succumb to the erotic enticement that his lips were promising. But she had to say it. The woman he thought she was would never let it go unmentioned.

'Have you any—protection?'

'Of course.'

He didn't even miss a beat. The response came as his caressing lips moved lower, found another pleasure spot Skye hadn't even known existed.

'The hotel shop stocks everything.'

'Oh, yes.'

She hoped she sounded more assured than she felt. She had had a desperate attack of nerves when he had approached Reception to register and with a muttered excuse had disappeared into the nearest Ladies to hide for a moment. By the time she had emerged, cheeks flushed brightly, he had been waiting for her by the bank of lifts, the room key in his hand.

'So now you can relax and know I'll take care of you.'

There was such a darkly sensuous undertone in that remark that it made her toes curl inside her shiny patent leather shoes. Suddenly wanting to be rid of even such minor restrictions, she kicked off the high-heeled pumps and relaxed into Anton's hold, abandoning herself to the moment. His arms almost lifted her off her feet, taking her up and hard against him so that she shivered at the feel of the hard ridge that marked the arousal he had no intention of hiding.

She flung her arms up around his neck, linking her fingers in the silky strands of the black hair as she gave herself up to the kiss. It was hard and hot and hungry and it fuelled an answering need inside her until she was burning up with it, swimming on a heated flood tide of passion.

Skye had never known her body to feel so alive before. Her heart was thudding, her head spinning. Her breasts felt swollen and, oh, so sensitive, the tight buds of her nipples stinging sharply.

She was swung off her feet, lifted from the floor and carried the short distance to the bed. Laying her down gently on the blue and green quilted covering, he kept his mouth on hers while his wickedly enticing hands found the fastenings of her dress, dispensing with the buttons in moments, the delicate lace of her bra no protection at all from his burning gaze.

Or the touch of those knowing hands.

At the sensation of the heat of his palms on her breasts, stroking delicately over the peach-coloured lace, catching and rolling the hardened nipples between strong fingers, Skye's eyes flew open, meeting the glittering black gaze of the man above her.

'An—' she began, but he silenced her once more, kissing the exclamation from her trembling mouth.

'Close your eyes,' he commanded against her lips. 'Close them and keep them shut.'

He caught her uncertain, anxious gaze and lifted his head to kiss her eyelids closed again, returning her to the warm velvet darkness once more.

'Don't look, just feel.'

How could she do anything else when already those tormenting hands were easing her bra from her, tracing hot, erotic patterns across her breasts, circling the peaks, making the nipples strain against their touch?

'Feel this...' he muttered with another tormenting caress

across the sensitised skin, trailing fiery paths that sent shock waves of sensation pulsing through her.

The gentleness was not enough. She wanted—needed—more! Blindly reaching for him, she closed her hands over his powerful shoulders, pulling him down towards her, crushing her lips to his.

'Help me—show me...' she began against his mouth, only realising just in time what she had almost given away, revealing herself to him more than she truly wanted to.

She didn't want him to realise—or even to suspect—her innocence. What would a man as sophisticated and worldly as this Anton seemed want with an innocent fresh up from the country—a real country bumpkin who had never known how it felt to make love with a man? An innocent whose lack of experience would no doubt make him laugh or shake his head in disbelief.

This man didn't want an untutored lover. He must be used to women as knowing and as experienced as he clearly was. She would die of embarrassment if he realised how far from experienced she was.

'Show me how to please you,' she amended hastily, hoping she had caught the betraying words soon enough.

'You're doing okay all by yourself,' was the muttered response and the raw edge to his voice made her heart jerk in unexpected sensual triumph.

Perhaps with her eyes closed she could be the woman he would want. With her eyes closed she felt less inhibited, less self-conscious. With her eyes closed she could indulge her need to reach out and touch, to let her hands close over the tight muscles of his shoulders and arms under the fine linen of his shirt.

When had he shrugged off his jacket?

Even working blind, her fingers had no problem dealing with the buttons down the front of his shirt, and within moments her searching hands had found the hot, hair-roughened skin of his chest. It felt so warm to her touch, the tingling excitement tantalising her, driving her to explore further—much to Anton's delight, to judge by his groan of response.

'Quite okay…'

'You're not doing badly either.'

Somehow she managed to find just the right, casual tone. She was stunned to realise that he had slipped her clothing from her without any of the awkward tugging and pulling she had anticipated. The air of the overheated hotel room was warm on her exposed flesh, and, keeping her eyes closed, she managed not to blush hotly at the realisation that those dark, deep-set eyes were now fixed on her near naked body.

But she couldn't ignore the fact of his touch. Her heart leapt at the first brush of hard fingers on delicate skin and it was all she could do not to curl up into a defensive ball and, muttering, 'Oh, don't,' try to hide away from him.

The sensation only lasted a moment. A couple of heart-shuddering seconds later she was relaxing into the wonderful sensations his caresses woke in her. Her hungry senses stirred, thrilled, cried out for more. And the whimpering cries that were all she could manage spoke to him only too clearly of her need.

The stroking hands grew harder, urgent, more demanding. And as she writhed beneath his touch his mouth moved over her too, kissing his way along her shoulder, down to the slope of her breast, catching the already aching nipple between his lips and tugging hard.

Skye's only response was a high, wordless sound of wonder as her breath stilled in her throat and her body arched against his in urgent invitation.

'Please…'

It was all she could manage, though she had no idea whether she was begging for more of the sharply sensual caress—or for him to stop before she fainted away completely from a pleasure that was so intense it was almost a pain. Burning sensations of delight sizzled through her, making her head spin, and the spiralling delight took all her ability to think from her.

Those wickedly tormenting hands were heading lower, stroking up the soft inner flesh of her thighs, slipping under the waist of the peach silk knickers that were somehow her only item of clothing, easing the flimsy garment away from her body.

All the embarrassment she had thought that she would feel at being exposed in this way was swept away on a molten tide of hunger. This was what she wanted; what she needed. This was…

Her mind splintered in an explosion of erotic delight as that tormenting touch reached the most sensitive spot of her femininity. The tantalising caress had her gasping in uncontrolled response, moving convulsively, stretching to press herself against that arousing fingertip. Wave after wave of heated pleasure throbbed through her, leaving her weak and abandoned, adrift on the aftershocks of a pleasure she had never known existed.

And in that moment Anton covered her body with his own, fitting his heavy, muscled legs between the splayed whiteness of her thighs, pushing them wide. The hot power of his erection sought the warm, slick darkness of her innermost core, and there was no time for hesitation or for fear. No time to suffer second thoughts or worry about her inexperience.

The actual moment of possession was so swift, so sure, thrusting deep into her already yearning body that only the faintest sting of pain, of protest from the stretching of tender tissues, gave any indication that this was the first experience of an unknown sensation. For just a brief heartbeat her eyes flew open wide, staring up into the dark, intent face above her in stunned bewilderment, blurring into a wild kaleidoscope of misty colour. Dazed grey gaze locked with passion-glazed black and the rest of the world went completely out of focus.

But then he began to move, deep and strong within her; each thrust piling sensation upon sensation, fire upon fire, until she thought her mind would surely melt in the inferno of pleasure that assailed her.

Her eyes fell closed again, the better to enjoy the stunning sensations rippling through her body. Her head went back against the pillows, her mouth slightly open to enable her to catch the breaths that seemed to have abandoned her needy lungs, her whole system going into shutdown, into primitive total concentration on the one vital core of her being.

She was being taken up and up again, lifted higher, higher, higher—climbing towards the peak she hadn't known existed, but had somehow, intuitively, instinctively, been reaching for. And in the instant that at last she reached it she toppled over the edge, no longer inside her body but floating high and free on a wild explosion of starlight, tumbling into complete oblivion, into the blank unconsciousness of total ecstasy.

A heartbeat later, Theo joined her, his harsh cry of fulfilment the last sound before he too lost all consciousness of the world apart from this woman whose body enclosed his so hotly, and the ragged, thudding beat of his own heart.

It was an unconsciousness from which he barely surfaced long into the night. There were times when his senses struggled to the surface of the erotic stupor into which he had fallen, and almost regained the knowledge of reality and where he was.

Almost.

Because each time he came close to waking, each time he stirred and reached out a hand or moved a sensually aching limb, he encountered the soft, warm shape of the woman beside him. And each time he touched her it was like connecting with a live electric current. The wildfire magic flared again, rousing them both from the depths of sleep, making them hungry again, setting their pulses pounding, their breath rasping. Bringing them together in a wild, fierce coupling that once again obliterated thought or any sense beyond the primitive demands of their bodies and the appetites that only each other could appease.

Until in the end a total exhaustion claimed them, dropping him down into a sleep so deep, so all-enclosing, that he didn't even stir when, just as dawn was breaking, Skye managed to drag herself from the depths of oblivion and forced her reluctant body to slip from the bed.

She couldn't even look at the sleeping man as she pulled on her clothes with more haste than finesse though she was painfully, agonisingly aware of his dark head, the powerfully carved features still resting on the softness of the pillows. She didn't want to leave. Tears stung her eyes at the thought of the moment that she would step outside the door of this small room—this small, uninteresting, anonymous room that had come to seem like a tiny piece of heaven to her. She would have to walk out that door, out of the glorious dream she had known for one night, and back into the cold, cruel world of life.

Reality would close around her once again and this very special time would just be a memory.

She didn't even dare press the kiss she hungered for on his sleeping face for fear that even the lightest touch would wake him. That those deep, dark eyes—the eyes she had lost herself in last night—would fly open and look straight into hers. She could almost see the frown that would crease the space between the black, arched brows, hear his softly accented voice demanding to know where she was going.

She couldn't face that. It would destroy her even to try.

Another day; another time. The words echoed like a lament inside her head.

If they had met another day, another time, then perhaps they might have had a future. She might have been able to—

No!

Fiercely she caught back her wayward thoughts, knowing they would weaken her resolve, tie her already leaden feet to the ground if she let them into her head.

She had to go—now—as fast as she could. Not even troubling to pull on tights over her bare legs, she forced her feet into her shoes, snatched up her jacket and bag, and fled towards the door.

There was a long desperate moment of panic as the handle squeaked, the hinges creaked, but then she was out and easing the door shut, allowing herself only a moment for a gasping sigh of relief before she fled down the carpeted corridor, heading for the lift.

Had she forgotten anything? Left a betraying clue behind?

A desperate check of her belongings confirmed she had everything with her—a fact that should have reassured her, but it didn't.

Because the truth was that what she had left behind was a vital part of her soul.

CHAPTER FOUR

'WE'LL be landing in five minutes, sir.'

'Thank you.'

Theo acknowledged his pilot's words with a nod. He hadn't even needed them, really. His own eyes had told him just how close they were getting to Helikos, the small dot in the ocean that was his father's private island.

The island that had been home to Theo himself, all the time he had been growing up.

Then, when he had been just a boy, and had returned home from the long weeks away at the exclusive English boarding-school he had detested but which his father had been determined would turn him into a gentleman, he had recognised every tiny landmark on the flight from Athens airport. He had almost hung out of the helicopter cockpit to spot each change in the scene beneath them, the dozens of other, tiny, uninhabited islands that marked the familiar route to his beloved family home.

And when Helikos had finally come into view, at first as just a small dot on the horizon, he had always let out a great cheer to celebrate that, at last, for him, the holidays had begun.

But this time there was no excited thudding of his heart, no resounding cheer on his lips. Instead he viewed the approaching coastline with a dour, cynical expression, watching it come nearer with a complicated mix of emotions in his soul. He was heading back to Helikos after an absence of five long years, but the island was no longer truly home to him. The split with his father had seen to that. And now there was the new wife to consider, too.

Theo scowled as the sound of the engine changed subtly, indicating that the pilot was beginning their descent. Another complication he could well do without. Though, from the little information he had had about her, this marriage was clearly not a love match. More like a business deal.

'I don't think you'll find the island much changed.'

It was the pilot again, interrupting his thoughts as his voice came through the earphones both men wore.

'I doubt if it's changed in the least.'

Theo kept his eyes on the dark mass of land set in the brilliant sea. He was not in the mood for conversation; in fact he was not in the mood to be here at all. He most definitely was not in the mood for meeting his father's latest floozy and trying to be polite to her. Cyril Antonakos was not known for choosing the most intelligent of female companions, and unless his father had changed dramatically in the past five years, then tonight's dinner when he was to meet the brand-new Antonakos bride-to-be was going to be a long endurance test.

All the more so because his mind would be anywhere but here on Helikos.

From the moment that he had woken to find the space in the bed beside him cold, the room empty, he hadn't been able to get the mysterious Skye out of his thoughts. He had spent the last week hunting for traces of the woman who had shared that one amazing night with him, but, with so little to go on, he had had a frustrating lack of success. He would do better, he knew, to forget the whole thing and put her out of his mind.

But in one brief night she had got completely under his skin and he couldn't forget about her. Even when he slept, his dreams were filled with hot, erotic images of the night they had spent together. He would dream that he held her close, her slender, smooth-skinned limbs entangled with his, her Titian hair spread across the pillows, over his face, her perfume driving him wild.

And then he'd wake with his heart racing, his breath coming in raw, uneven gasps, his body slicked with sweat as if he had actually been making love to her in reality and not just in his mind. But of course none of it was real— none of it except the burning ache in his groin, the throb of unappeased hunger through every nerve.

If he could, he would have made some excuse and not come here. But the division between him and his father had gone on quite long enough. If Cyril was prepared to offer an olive branch, however half-hearted, then he, Theo, would meet him more than part way.

The house was just as he remembered it. High on a cliff above the sea, the huge white building sprawled over a large plot of land on two levels, each with its own vast veranda giving an amazing view of the ocean. A wide arched gateway to one side led to a stone-flagged patio, the oval swimming pool, and a small pool house that doubled as a guest house.

As Theo approached the door was pulled open and a small, plump, dark-haired figure hurried towards him.

'Master Theo! Welcome! It's wonderful to have you back!'

'Amalthea…'

Theo submitted to the exuberant embrace of the tiny woman who had been his nurse as he grew up, and, because his mother had died when he was small, the closest person to a mother he had ever known.

'Where am I staying? Have you put me in my old room?'

Amalthea's dark eyes clouded as she shook her greying head.

'Your father told me to put you in the pool house.'

So the olive branch was not quite as definite as he had thought, Theo told himself with a twist of sardonic resignation. His father was a hard man to like—a difficult man to love. He took offence easily and held onto grudges for a long, long time. It seemed that being invited here for the old man's wedding was only the start of things. There wasn't any sign of the fatted calf being prepared for the return of the prodigal son.

'Who's in my room?'

Surely the guests hadn't started to arrive just yet? The wedding wasn't taking place until the end of the month.

'The new *Kyria* Antonakos.'

'My father's fiancée?'

So his father and the bride-to-be didn't share a room already. That was a surprise.

'What's she like?'

Amalthea rolled her eyes in an expression of disapproval that she could only get away with in front of Theo.

'Not at all his usual sort. But she is very beautiful.'

'They're always beautiful,' Theo commented cynically. 'That's why he chooses them. Is my father at home now?'

'He had to go to the village,' Amalthea told him. 'But he'll be back this evening in time for dinner. His fiancée is at home. Would you want to—'

'Oh, no,' Theo put in swiftly, before she could even form the suggestion. 'Dinner time will be soon enough.'

That way he could get both awkward encounters over and done with in the same time. Perhaps making polite small talk with The Fiancée would be easier than trying to carry on any sort of a conversation with his parent.

'My bags will have been taken to the pool house. I'll unpack and settle in—maybe have a swim.'

He stretched slowly, easing muscles cramped tight after the journey from London.

'It's good to be home.'

So this was to be home.

Skye turned away from the window with its panoramic

view of the sea and sank back down onto the bed with a sigh, digging her teeth into her lower lip in an attempt to force back the tears that were threatening.

She was always on the edge of tears these days. Always only just managing to subdue the panic that gripped her when she contemplated what lay ahead of her. She still couldn't quite take it all in. Still couldn't believe that this was to be her future.

But sitting here brooding wasn't going to change that. She really ought to come out of the bedroom at some point soon, and get to know the rest of the house better. She was going to live here, after all.

That thought only added to her sense of desolate unreality. This house, beautiful as it was, just didn't seem anything like the home she had left in the damp and green countryside of Suffolk, the small village where she had grown up.

She supposed she would get used to it in time. She *had* to get used to it; she had no choice.

Skye rubbed the back of her hand across her eyes, brushing away the tears. When she'd phoned home earlier, her father had told her that her mother had been taken into hospital again. Claire Marston needed yet another operation, and soon. And her doctors had said that it was vital she was kept quiet. Any stress at all could be fatal.

It was a terrible, bitter irony, one that brought a taste like the burn of acid into her mouth, to think that she had always dreamed of visiting Greece, of seeing the cluster of the Sporades Islands, perhaps holidaying there. She had dreamed of the sunshine, the sea, the white houses she had seen in photographs. And now she had achieved her dream, but it had turned into a terrible nightmare; one from which even waking wouldn't mean that she could escape.

Now she had the sun. It had been shining all day. And,

there, beyond her window, was the sea, an almost unbelievable bright and sparkling turquoise in colour. She lived
in one of the white houses—a *huge* white house. And she
hated it.

She was lonely and lost and terrified of the future.

And she had no way out.

'Oh, Dad! Why did you have to be so stupid? How could
you have made such a mess of things?'

If only…

But no! Skye caught herself up sharply, giving herself a
brusque, reproving shake.

She couldn't let herself dwell on *if only*. Couldn't even
let herself dream of *if only*.

But, oh, *if only* she had never made that mad, foolish
mistake last week. If only she hadn't given into the crazy,
wild impulse to have one last night of freedom while she
could.

And *if only* she had never met the most devastating man
called Anton. A man who had taken her to bed for the most
amazing, most stunning, most memorable night of passion.
The only night of such passion she was ever likely to know.
A night of passion she would never forget.

And she could never, *ever* forget the man who had shared
it with her.

But because she would never forget, then the situation
in which she now found herself became so very much
worse. Appallingly so. Perhaps before last week she might
have been able to bear the prospect of the future with some
degree of equanimity. Now she had been shown, oh, so
briefly, the image of another, very different future, only to
have it snatched away from her for ever, and she had no
idea at all how she was ever going to cope.

But she had to. Even though she felt that her heart would
break just with trying.

'Come on, Marston!' she told herself fiercely. 'Pull your-

self together. You're going to have to make the best of
this!'

She could at least keep herself busy. Keep her mind occupied and not let herself brood.

What was it Cyril had said before he left—to go into the
village on business?

'Make yourself at home. The house is yours—anything
you want, just ask for it. Use the cinema, or the pool.'

The pool! There was her answer. Some exercise would
distract her; it would fill the long, empty afternoon that
stretched ahead. And if she was lucky, it would tire her out
so that she would finally manage to sleep tonight.

And she needed to sleep, she told herself as she pulled
open a drawer, hunting through it for the sleek white costume that Cyril had insisted on buying for her when he had
realised that she didn't have anything to wear to swim in,
apart from the regulation navy blue one piece that had seen
her through school and was now definitely on its last legs.

She would exercise until she was exhausted and then
tonight she might crash out, almost unconscious. With luck
she would not have to lie there, in the strange bed, staring
at the white-painted ceiling, remembering…

Or would falling asleep be worse? Every night she had
slept so badly, locked in feverish dreams of a night in a
hotel, a long, sleekly muscled body next to hers, powerful
arms holding her, jet-black eyes looking down at her. And
every morning she had woken with the bedclothes in a
twisted tangle, knotted around her body, evidence of the
disturbed night she had passed.

She was shivering with reaction to her memories as she
pulled on the white swimsuit, grabbed a towel, and headed
for the pool.

Theo's unpacking only took a very short time. There was
little enough to put away in the cupboards of the pool house

where his father had left instructions he was to stay, his old room apparently being occupied by The Fiancée, and now he was at a loss. The afternoon was warm and the thought of the cool, clear water of the pool was appealing. It was the work of seconds to change into black swimming shorts and head outside, padding silently in bare feet over the white-tiled surround.

What he didn't expect was to see someone already in the water. Shock brought him to a halt, eyes narrowing against the glint of the sun on the water as he studied the scene before him.

A sleek form sped through the water, powering from one end of the pool to another. A sleek *female* form in a clinging white costume. The Fiancée, if he wasn't very much mistaken. He couldn't see much of her from here, she was swimming away from him and the water hid most of her body. He had a brief, blurred impression of dark hair, long, slender arms slicing through the water, slim, toned legs kicking out behind the shapely body, high, tight buttocks...

What the *hell* was he doing? He couldn't have thoughts like that about his father's fiancée—the woman who was going to be his stepmother by the end of the month.

Or was this in fact the brand-new fiancée? Because she was much younger than he had ever anticipated...

Perhaps The Fiancée had been married before and this girl was a daughter? Whoever she was, she made him think disturbingly of the mysterious Skye.

He'd better make himself known to her. He didn't want to give the impression of behaving like a peeping Tom, standing here staring at her.

'*Kalimera.*'

She hadn't heard him—the water must still be in her ears. Or perhaps she didn't even understand Greek. A cynical smile twisted his mouth. It was an indication of just how bad things had become between him and his father that he had no idea whether the new woman in Cyril's life was Greek or some other nationality entirely. The last time he had known anything about any of Cyril's mistresses, his father had been deeply involved with a woman from the village.

'Good afternoon.' He spoke again, more firmly and clearly this time, just as she reached the far end of the pool and held onto the side, wiping the water from her face. 'I think I ought to introduce myself to you, Stepmama.'

It was her stillness that told him something was wrong. The sudden total freezing into immobility that caught on a raw edge in his mind and made him frown, studying her more closely.

Just what had he said that had startled her so much?

Even from this distance he could see the way that she clutched at the side of the pool, the pressure that turned the knuckles white on each delicate hand.

That hand…

Suddenly, shockingly, it was as if he had been kicked in the stomach hard.

A cold, damp night in London. A smoky bar. The laughter of two men.

A hand held prisoner on the table top.

'*Theos*, no!'

He had to be imagining things. Fooling himself.

But in the warmth of the Greek sun the hair that tumbled down her back—the hair that he had thought was dark, but now he could see was only soaked with water from the pool—was already starting to dry. And as it dried its colour changed, lightening…revealing a red-gold tint.

'*Ochi*…'

Feeling as if he had been slapped on the side of the head, Theo reverted to his native Greek, shaking his head in denial of what he was seeing, what he suspected.

'No!'

It couldn't be true.

But if it wasn't, then why was she still standing as if frozen, with her head turned away from him—that long, straight back held tight with tension, the delicate hands clenched over the edge of the pool?

Why didn't she turn and face him—revealing the features of a total stranger, shattering the foolish, damn stupid, appalling delusion that had taken a grip on his mind and wouldn't let go?

She wasn't…she *couldn't* be…

'Skye?'

From the moment that she had first heard that voice, Skye had been fixed to the spot, unable to move, unable to think, unable to breathe.

'Good afternoon,' he had said, and it was as if a cruel hand had reached out through time and yanked her backwards, dragging her away from the present, and back into the past, into a whirlwind of memories that paralysed her mind, slashed at her soul.

'Good afternoon.'

Those were the words she had heard in the clear light of today. But in her mind what she had heard was: *Oh, but he does.*

The first words that Anton had spoken on the night in London. The night that ever since had simply become *that night* in her thoughts, with no further title needed.

That night.

That was when she had first heard that rich, slightly husky voice with the touch of the beautiful accent that made her toes curl in response.

But how could she have heard it here and now?

She had to be imagining things! She couldn't have heard it. He couldn't be here. Fate couldn't be so cruel.

But then he had said, 'I think I ought to introduce myself

to you,' and the world had tilted violently, swinging right off balance, making her head spin crazily.

Her vision had blurred, her stomach had clenched tight in panic. She couldn't see, couldn't think. She *had* to know—and yet she didn't dare to look round, terrified in case she was right. In case it *was* him.

And then the worst horror of all.

'Skye?'

He used her name. In the voice that she had heard him use dozens of times—a hundred times—on *that night.* She had heard it said calmly, heard it said softly, heard it said huskily, seductively, passionately, demandingly. And finally, she had heard her own name used as a cry of fulfilment, as he had lost himself in her. But always, always, in that voice.

Anton?

She didn't dare to speak his name aloud, fearing that she might be tempting fate by doing so. That she might turn into reality what she still fervently hoped was just a delusion, a trick of sound combining with her overactive imagination.

'What the hell?'

The harsh, angry question brought her swinging round, unable to bear the suspense any longer. She *had* to know.

He was standing on the edge of the pool, hands on hips. The sun was behind him so that she had to squint against it to see his face. But she already knew, and her heart was racing so fast that she was sure it would escape the confines of her chest. Already she couldn't breathe and her mind was frozen in stunned horror.

Perhaps it was because of that, or perhaps it was the sun dazzling her eyes, but something made her lose her grip, slip and fall. She reached for the rim of the pool, missed, and went under, still gasping for breath.

Water in her ears and eyes, she didn't hear anything, couldn't see anything. She went down...down...

There was a flurry nearby. A long body slashed into the water at her side. Strong hands seized her; powerful arms hauled her up to the surface. Before she had time to think, she was dragged to the shallow end of the pool, and supported gently as she gasped and wheezed, struggling to get her breath back.

'Steady,' that voice advised her. 'Breathe deeply.'

She would if she could, Skye told herself, but if anything was guaranteed *not* to calm her down, it was this.

Now she didn't have to look into his face to know he was Anton. Even after only one night—*that night*—she knew this male body so intimately that she could never mistake it. There were the hard, strong bones of the ribcage, the black curling hair that marked a path down the centre of his chest, disappearing under the waistband of the swimming trunks. There was the tiny, crescent shaped scar high up on his collar-bone, almost at the base of his throat. And if there had been any room for doubt, then her nostrils were filled with the scent of his body, musky, intensely male, warmed by the sun and blending with the ozone tang of the pool water.

She didn't know if it was her intense physical reaction to him or simply the shock of his sudden appearance that made her tremble all over, her legs feeling too weak to support her.

'Thank you,' she managed, her voice sounding as if she had been running a marathon.

'No problem,' he returned smoothly, though there was a dark thread to his voice that brought her head up sharply, frowning grey eyes meeting the fixed black gaze of his.

He didn't enlighten her further, but instead half dragged, half carried her to the low stone steps into the pool, swinging her up into his arms and carrying her out onto the tiled edge where he set her down again beside a wooden lounger.

Skye had to bite down hard on her lower lip to keep her mouth closed against the cry of protest as he let her go. In his arms, she had been struggling with a terrible longing, with a weak, dangerous impulse to turn her head into his chest and let it rest there. The need to nestle close into his arms, to put her own hands up around his neck and cling on tight, had almost overwhelmed her. But she had known that such a response was forbidden her. She had forfeited the right to it in the moment that she had closed the door on that hotel room and walked away.

He would never know just how hard she had found it to do that. How much she had longed to stay, but known that it was impossible. She had left a piece of her heart with him, though he would never know it. And as soon as he worked out just why she was here then he wouldn't even want her near him, let alone keep her in his arms where she longed to be.

Still supporting her with one hand, he snatched up a towel with the other and began to rub her dry. His movements were brisk and impersonal and the one, nervous look she shot at his face made her stomach tie itself into tight, painful knots of apprehension.

The stunning face was tight with control, skin drawn so taut over the forceful bone structure that it was actually white at the corners of his mouth with the effort of not speaking. He was only keeping quiet until she had recovered.

And then?

Just the thought made her shiver again, more violently this time, yelping in discomfort as he increased the pressure of the towel on her sensitised skin.

'*Sighnomi…*'

The apology was abstracted and he tossed the towel

away, coal-black eyes raking over her from the top of her head, where her wet hair hung in tangled rats' tails around her face, to the bare pink toes on the white-tiled surface.

But it was when they swung back up to her face that her courage almost failed her completely.

Now it was going to begin, she told herself, swallowing hard.

He'd waited long enough, that cold, set expression said. Now he wanted explanations.

CHAPTER FIVE

'WE HAVE some talking to do.'

Theo had no idea how he kept control over his voice. The coldly burning rage inside him would keep fighting to get away from his determination to rein it in, and the resulting conflict made his tone brutal and cold as a sword of ice.

He wanted to know just what the hell was going on. How the woman he had last seen in a London hotel room—the woman who had wanted only a one-night stand, no names, no information—had turned up on Helikos, at his father's house, in his father's pool.

Though he would be able to think much more clearly if she would just cover up.

'Don't you have a wrap or something? Something to put on.'

'I—I'm not cold.'

'It's not your temperature I was thinking of!'

He knew he was glaring ferociously. The look in her eyes and the way that she took an instinctive step backwards, away from him, told him that. But he had been knocked off balance by the discovery of her in the pool and being close to her, like this, only made matters so much worse.

He had thought that his memories of her soft-skinned, naked body were arousing enough—in fact, he had tried to convince himself that he had exaggerated her appeal. No woman, no real, living, breathing woman, could have been as physically appealing as his recollections told him she had been. But those recollections had been nothing but the truth.

Less than the truth, in fact. Because the memories had none of the warm, physical presence of this woman. And though the white swimming costume might be modest when compared with the skimpy bikinis worn by so many on the Greek beaches, its subtle sexuality was doing devastating things to his heart rate and his ability to think. The stretchy material clung to the swell of her breasts and hips, the thin straps revealing the peachy skin and soft curves of her shoulders, while the cutaway shape made her legs seem endlessly elegant. Just to think of those long legs curled around his waist, squeezing tight as she gave herself up to the throes of her orgasm, threatened to blow his mind into tiny, spinning splinters that were impossible to form into any coherent thoughts.

'We might both be able to talk more rationally if you were more—respectably dressed.'

That softly curved mouth took on a mutinous set that wasn't quite matched by the flare of something in her eyes. Not anger, but something wild and defiant, clashing with his dark glare until he almost felt he could see sparks in the air between them.

'And you think that your clothing is so much more decorous?' she flashed back, lacing the words with an unexpected sting.

'Is that a way of saying that you don't trust yourself to keep your hands off me?' Theo said scornfully. 'Because you'll have to forgive me if I don't believe you. You had no trouble tearing yourself away from my bed that night...'

'*That night* was a mistake and one I've regretted ever since.'

'Not as much as I have, lady. I don't happen to go in for one-night stands and if I'd known you were going to disappear like that, I'd have had more than second thoughts about the whole situation. And then when I find you swimming in my father's pool—'

'I never tried to deceive you in any way. I told you exactly what…'

Her voice died abruptly as she realised just what he had said. All colour fled from her cheeks, leaving her looking white as a ghost.

'Your *father's*—!'

She actually glanced back at the pool and then back to his face, her grey eyes wide with shock and disbelief.

'Did you say…?'

This couldn't be real! It couldn't be happening, Skye thought in desperation. Please let it not be happening. Please let it be a dream—a nightmare from which she could wake.

He couldn't have said *my father's pool*. Because that would make him Cyril's son. The son of the man she had to marry. The son of the man who held the fate of her whole family in his hands and who could destroy their hope of a future if he chose.

She actually caught a tiny part of her arm in her fingers and pinched hard, praying it might bring her out of the horror. But, of course, nothing happened. She was still standing there, bathed in the Greek sunlight, with the only sound that of a faint ripple of the water in the pool where a breeze hit it.

And Anton was standing beside her, big and dark and dangerous-looking.

'But you said your name was Anton.'

She flung the accusation into his cold, set face, but his expression didn't change and he continued to regard her with a stony lack of expression.

Anton…*Antonakos*. Suddenly the truth fell into place with a shock that made her head spin.

'You lied to me!'

His shrug was a swift, careless dismissal of the charge.

'I was economical with the truth. I find it's often the best policy until I get to know someone's real motives.'

The cold, slashing look he flung at her left her in no doubt that she had been included in the group of people whose motives he considered suspect. The ice in it seemed to take away all the heat of the sun so that her skin crawled with goose-bumps and it was all she could do to suppress an instinctive shiver. Reaching for the towel she had left on the wooden lounger earlier, she pulled it round her, knotting it securely over her breasts, under her armpits.

Covered, she felt a little more confident until he spoke again.

'And, as I recall, you were the one who insisted we kept to one name only.'

He was right, of course, and the knowledge of it didn't make her feel any better. Dear God, what sort of malign fate had brought her together with this man on that night? How had she had the appalling bad luck to walk into the one bar where Cyril's son had been sitting on his own?

And what had he been doing in London? All she knew about Cyril and his son was that they had not been on the best of terms for some time. So did this man know…?

The terrible reality of the whole truth she had been keeping from him made her stomach heave nauseously.

'Mine was at least my real one,' she said, taking the risk of stepping a little further into the danger zone. 'I'm Skye Marston.'

There was no flicker of anything in the opaque-eyed stare that he turned on her. So was it possible that his father hadn't told him?

'Theodore Antonakos,' he returned, totally deadpan. 'Usually known as Theo.'

The look that scoured over her made her feel as if it had scraped away a much-needed layer of skin, so that in spite of the bulky protection of the towel wrapped around her she felt exposed and naked to his cold scrutiny.

'So now what?' the man she now had to call Theo drawled with lazy mockery. 'Do we shake hands formally and really do everything totally back to front?'

'I think we'll take the handshake as read,' Skye returned stiffly. The idea of even touching him frankly terrified her. She just could not forget the burn of his skin on hers, the caressing touch of those long, powerful hands that could turn as gentle as the patting paws of a kitten when he chose or be as demanding as blazing fire. 'We've already done that bit.'

'And more,' he returned dryly, and the wicked gleam deep in those brilliant black eyes told her that he remembered every moment of it.

As did she.

That night was etched onto her brain in images of fire. It had been bad enough when it was just a memory. But now, with the man himself an actual physical force before her, not just an image in her mind, she felt as if her thoughts might go up in flames as a result.

'I'd rather forget about that.'

The tension in every inch of her body had affected her mouth too, and the words came out so tight and clipped they could hardly have been more stilted. Her voice sounded like some second-rate actress trying to speak like an upper-class Englishwoman, and strangling the sounds as she did so.

Evidently Theo thought so too, as his wide, mobile mouth twitched uncontrollably at her words. But every last trace of humour was erased from it when he spoke, and his eyes had turned to black ice under heavy, hooded lids.

'I'm sure you would, but I have to tell you that I don't feel the same.'

Provocatively he reached out a lazy hand and trailed his

fingers along her throat and across the top of the white towel, coming to a deliberate halt by the knot that held it closed.

'The truth is that the experience is one I would very much like to repeat.'

The bronzed fingertips moved to the edge of her shoulder, then back again, and it was all Skye could do to control the instinctive squirm of response that would have betrayed her feelings.

The instant peaking and hardening of her breasts was something she could do nothing about. A heat that had nothing to do with the sun, licked along her veins, making the towel seem too heavy, the clinging white swimming costume too restricting to wear underneath it. But she could only be thankful that the thick padding hid her intimate reaction from those probing black eyes.

'Then I'm afraid you'll have a long wait. I told you it was a one-night thing only.'

'You also told me that we would never know each other's names. Never meet again.'

He paused just long enough for the shocking impact of those words to hit home hard with the realisation that both of them had now been disproved.

'And *I* told you that I never do one-night stands. It's a personal rule I have.'

'Well, then, it's a rule that you're just going to have to break this time. Because I have no intention of renewing our—acquaintance in any way. One night was more than enough for me and that's the way I want things to stay.'

'Is that so?'

His arms folded across his chest, Theo looked her up and down with coldly contemptuous black eyes.

'Well, let's see.'

Before Skye had a moment to realise just what was in his thoughts, he had moved forward, taking her chin in one powerful hand and wrenching her face up towards his. She had just one split second in which to recognise the ruthless intent in his eyes, but not long enough to voice the protest that formed in her mind.

Her mouth was still opening to try and speak as his came down, hard and determined, crushing the objection straight back down her throat.

As a kiss, it was cruel and passionless, but as an act of punishment for rejecting his demand out of hand, it was perfect. There was nothing of affection or warmth in it, only a cold-blooded determination to show her who was in control here.

But it didn't stay that way.

Because something happened in the moment that their lips touched. Something that charged the atmosphere, changed the truth of that kiss into something very new and very different.

From something meant to control and be controlled, in the space of a heartbeat it flared into something totally *out* of control. Heat burned; hunger woke and demanded appeasement; need broke free of all restraint.

Skye swayed forwards, melting against Theo's hard form, and his arms came out to enclose her, imprison her along the length of him. Skin seemed to blend with skin, arms, legs, bodies entangled. Their heartbeats lurched, quickened, raced, thudding in time with each other, drowning out all other sounds beyond the pulse of molten blood in their veins. Their only breathing was the quickly snatched gasps of urgent passion, grabbed at frantically to avoid oblivion, but allowing for only the briefest moments away from the clinging, teasing, openly demanding mouth of the other.

'Skye—beauty—*agape mou…*'

Theo's voice was thick and rough with lust, his hands as clumsy as they tugged at the barrier of soft towelling that came between them, pulling the insecure knot loose in seconds, the white folds tumbling to the ground at their feet.

'You may have had enough but I have not. I want this—'

Skye's mouth opened under his in a gasp of shocked delight as his hand skimmed over her straining body, heat searing through the white Lycra, inflaming her hunger even more.

'And I want this…'

That searching hand found the swell of one breast where the betraying nipple pulsed against the restraint of the clinging material, his thumb catching and circling the hardened bud, making her moan aloud in wild expression of her need.

'Oh, yes, this.'

It was a low, dark undertone, with fiendish laughter running through it. Laughter that darkened even further as his urgent fingers tugged at the strap of her costume, wrenching it down over her shoulder, imprisoning her arm against her side and exposing the white slope of her upper breast.

While the hard warmth of his hand supported the soft weight, his hungry mouth sought the exposed flesh, kissing, licking, even nipping lightly at the smooth skin until Skye flung back her head and moaned aloud.

'This is what I want,' he muttered harshly against her. 'And it's what you want too. What we both want more than all the world. It's what's between us, lady. You can't fight it, and neither can I.'

The only response Skye could manage was a wild, indeterminate sound that could have been either acceptance or denial, but clearly Theo took it as acceptance.

'Come with me, my lovely. Come with me now…'

'No!'

Skye had no idea just what it was that jolted her out of the heated fantasy into which she'd fallen. She didn't know if it was some faint, unexpected sound that intruded in her mental delirium, or the way that Theo's mouth had left her breast or the sudden cooling touch of a tiny breeze that wafted its way across her exposed skin. She only knew that some unexpected sneaking coldness had slipped into her mind, dousing the heat that raged, stunning her into shocked realisation of just what she was doing.

'I said no!'

Desperation gave her a strength she hadn't known she possessed so that she could push him away, hard, the force of the movement driving him almost to the edge of the pool. But he recovered in a second, whirling back to face her, black eyes glittering in cold rage.

'What do you mean—?'

'Oh, come on!'

The frantic tattoo her heart was beating at the thought of the narrow escape she had just had, the shivering sensation brought by the realisation of how close she had come to total disaster, made Skye's voice range up and down in panic, but at least she sounded strong enough and determined enough to make him stop and listen to her.

'What part of no don't you understand? You may be Greek, *Kyrios* Antonakos, but your English isn't as bad as that. You know exactly what I meant!'

'I know what you *said*,' Theo flung back venomously. 'But that isn't exactly what you *meant*. And I don't need to know any English at all to differentiate between the two. I have other ways of interpreting that.'

'Other ways?'

For a moment Skye simply gaped in blank confusion, but then he gave a slow, deliberate glance from those polished jet eyes, away from her face and dropping down to rest on her still-exposed breast—and the betraying tightness of the pouting nipple, blatant evidence to anyone who wanted to look of the hunger he had roused in her. A hunger that was still clawing at her insides, making it almost impossible to think beyond the burning sense of need.

But she *had* to think. She had to stop feeling and force her mind to concentrate on what really mattered. She had almost ruined everything. Almost destroyed her chances of rescuing her family from the total disaster that faced them. The man before her, tall and strong, with the sunlight playing on the silken black hair, the bronzed skin of his face and chest, might be everything she most wanted in the world right now, but she had to force that weak, indulgent feeling from her mind and *think*.

And what she had to think was that this must not, could not, happen.

If she wanted to save her family, then Theo Antonakos was forbidden to her.

And so she wrenched up the dangling strap of the swimming costume, wincing in distress as the white Lycra scraped over the sensitised tip of her aching breast. Pulling the little clothing she had as high as it would go, she forced herself to face Theo's cold-eyed fury with what she hoped looked like a degree of calm she was far from feeling.

'I don't give a damn about your "other ways"!' she managed, the brutal control she was exerting over her voice making it sound high and tight, and absolutely cold with rejection. 'The one thing you listen to is what I *say*! And what I say is *no*—got that? N-O. No! I'm saying no and I *mean* no.'

For one fearful second there was such a maelstrom of rage in his face, blazing in his eyes, that she actually feared he would ignore her and reach out, grab her once again. She had nerved herself for flight when she saw him recollect himself, shake his head faintly and impose a degree of control over his actions that she had to admire even as she welcomed it with a shaking rush of relief.

But if Theo had controlled his physical impulses, he had not yet restrained his tongue.

'You say that now, sweetheart,' he declared with brutal

cynicism, 'but that no was a long time coming. So tell me, my lovely, what was it that forced the rejection from you? Was it the thought that someone else might see us—your mama perhaps?'

'Mama?' Skye echoed blankly, unable to believe he had used the word. Had he really said…?

'Because if that's what it was, my angel, then I'm certain you don't need to worry. I'm sure she'd be perfectly happy for us both.'

'Happy?'

Just what was he talking about? Every word confused her even more. What had her mother to do with this? Did Theo know…?

'Keep it in the family, so to speak. Your mother, my father—you and me.'

Your mother, my father…

Skye's thoughts reeled sickeningly. He thought her mother was his father's fiancée! He actually believed that she was here with her mother and that her mother was the one about to marry Cyril Antonakos!

'Well?'

Skye's silence, the stunned look on her face, puzzled Theo. Defiance he could understand; even anger would be perfectly explicable. But all the anger that had burned in her seemed to have fizzled out, subsiding like a damp squib that had never actually exploded.

And in a way that disappointed him.

He was spoiling for a fight. Had been ever since she had tried to claim that she didn't want him any more. It stung his pride to hear her declare that, especially when a tension in the sexy body in the clinging white swimsuit and a particular light in the depths of those dove-grey eyes revealed the statement for the lie that it was.

She couldn't have been more aware of him if she had been a nervous young deer who had come upon a hunting tiger in the middle of a clearing. She seemed unaware of the way that she was uneasily shifting her weight from one foot to another, her eyes warily watching his slightest move. Even the fine nostrils seemed to flare in apprehension every time he moved or spoke.

Like hell, she'd had enough of him! Just as there was no way that he had ever tired of her.

Anger and hurt pride had pushed him into action, making him pull her close. And her reaction had been everything that he had anticipated. Everything he had wanted. She had turned to flames in his arms, going up like the driest of kindling laid at the base of a fire, her passion so fierce that he had almost felt his skin might have melted in the heat of it. She had responded to his kiss with all the hunger and the desire that he'd dreamed of.

And he had been lost. Swamped by heat and desire; his body hardening in a second. He had lost all awareness of where he was.

He had thought that he had taken her along with him. Her responses had been everything he could have wanted, her kisses adding fuel to the fires blazing within him. He had been so sure that she was his. That once more he would have her in his bed—and that this time he would make sure it was for much longer than one night.

One night with her had already taught him that it was nowhere near long enough to sate himself on her body. One night had only made him realise what hunger really was and how much he wanted this woman in his bed. Finding her here like this, after his vain search for her in London, had been such an unexpected thrill and he was prepared to do whatever it took to keep her here.

The fight, the tension between them had only added to the electrical current of desire that sparked his appetite for her. And her sudden rejection of him, the way she had

pulled away, had left him fiercely frustrated, his aroused
body ready to take the satisfaction it needed.

Now she had just backed down.

Apparently with nothing to say, she was simply staring
at him as if he had suddenly grown an extra head, her big
eyes wide and clouded with something that looked like
shock.

'Well?' he repeated. 'What do you say?'

'I…' she began, but her voice trailed off, dying into silence once again.

Theo's hands clamped tight shut at his sides, struggling
to resist the urge to shake her from this trance she seemed
to have fallen into.

'Skye!'

But as he spoke another voice came from the direction
of the house, breaking into what he had been about to say
and silencing him too.

'Theo! There you are! Amalthea said you had arrived.'

Taken by surprise, Theo muttered a dark curse under his
breath. His father's appearance was the last thing he wanted
right now.

After five years' estrangement, not speaking, not even
sending letters, this first meeting with Cyril was going to
be awkward enough without anyone else there. The presence of someone else—and just who that someone was—
was a complication he could do without.

'*Pateras.*'

A sudden movement drew his eyes from the dark, heavy-
set man now approaching and back to Skye. She had
snatched up the white towel from the ground and was once
more knotting it hastily round her body. Such unexpected
modesty on her part frankly surprised him. And so did her
sudden loss of colour. Every trace of blood had ebbed from
her cheeks, leaving her looking strained and almost ill, the
wide grey eyes huge pools above the ashen cheeks.

'Skye?'

It came out on an undertone of concern, keeping the low-voiced question from his father's hearing. Theo knew better than most that the older man could be difficult and autocratic in his business dealings and with other men. But with women—particularly young, attractive women—he was usually a practised charmer, unlikely to cause such a panic-stricken reaction in any member of the opposite sex.

So was there some tension between his father and Skye Marston that he knew nothing about? It was going to make for an awkward relationship between Cyril and his about-to-be stepdaughter if that was the case.

But Skye had already turned away from him and was watching Cyril's approach, her face hidden so that he couldn't read any further changes in her expression.

'So you two have met already.'

If there was something wrong, then clearly Cyril wasn't aware of it as he directed a smile straight into Skye's face. His greeting of his son was more restrained, his expression several degrees short of warm, but he took the hand that Theo offered him and shook it hard.

'Good to have you back under my roof again, boy.'

That 'boy' grated as Theo was sure it was supposed to. His father had never accepted that he had grown up long ago. That had been one of the reasons for their estrangement.

But he had promised himself that this time he would really try to keep the peace.

'I couldn't miss the wedding,' he said, unable to erase the stiffness from his tone.

'Of course not. And you had to meet your new step-mother—which I see you've already done.'

Already done?

Thoughts spinning, Theo tried to force the words to make

sense, but failed completely. There was no logic to them—not unless…

Hell—no! His mind revolted at the thought. He refused to accept the way he was thinking. It was impossible—had to be.

But his father's arm had gone around Skye's waist, and he was turning her round to face his son. 'Still, I'll do the formal introductions now.'

No! Theo wanted to shout it at the top of his voice to drown out what was coming. He wanted to put his hands over his father's mouth to stop him speaking—anything—stem the flow of words that seemed to be leading inexorably to the most appalling conclusion.

It couldn't be—*Theos,* let it not be possible.

But Skye's cheeks seemed to have grown even paler. And her huge light grey eyes looked anywhere but into his face as his father continued blithely with his announcement, totally unaware of the impact it was having.

'Theo, I want you to meet Skye Marston, soon to be Skye Antonakos. Your new stepmother-to-be and, of course, my fiancée.'

CHAPTER SIX

IF LOOKS could kill then she would have died a thousand times over tonight, Skye thought miserably as she tried once more to make a pretence of eating the meal that had been put in front of her. The cold blaze of fury in the black eyes of the man sitting opposite felt as if it had the power to shrivel her into nothing where she sat, reducing her to just a small bundle of ashes on her chair.

She wished that the earth would just open and swallow her up, anything so that she didn't have to be here. She would much rather have escaped to her room and stayed hidden there all night.

But there was no escape. Cyril Antonakos liked a formal dinner in the evenings and he expected his family and guests to dress up for it. So she had been forced to put on the elegant peacock-blue silk dress he had told her to wear, pin her hair up into an elegant roll at the back of her head and sit down at the big wooden table to endure the worst sort of torture by food.

She had no idea at all what she was supposed to be eating, only that it had as much taste and texture as stewed sawdust and that it was impossible to swallow anything because her throat seemed to have closed up completely.

And the all the time Theo Antonakos was watching her like a hawk eyeing its prey, watching, waiting, judging the best time to swoop down and pounce. And just like some tiny, shivering dormouse cowering on the ground and watching the shadow of the predator's wings circling over-head, she had no doubt that when he did decide to act, then the attack would be swift, merciless—and totally lethal.

She was just surprised that he hadn't denounced her to his father from the first moment he had realised who she was. She had fully expected the condemnation to come as soon as the introduction had been made and her heart had stopped beating, her breath catching in her throat as she'd waited for the words that would ruin her and her family and bring the whole delicate structure of Cyril's unexpected offer to rescue them tumbling down around her.

But to her astonishment it hadn't happened. Somehow Theo had controlled the burn of fury deep inside him, though, seeing the anger that had blazed in his eyes, Skye had recognised that it was there and only the most savage and ruthless control was what held it back, kept it from showing in his voice when he had replied to his father's introduction.

'Ms Marston and I had just made ourselves known to each other,' he said smoothly. So smoothly that Skye actually blinked hard in shock at the skilful way he managed to fake an easy calm that he was clearly so very far from feeling. 'You're a lucky man, Father, to have such a beautiful fiancée.'

And then, when she was least expecting it, and when she certainly wasn't at all emotionally prepared, he shocked her rigid by holding out his hand to her in a pretence of a formal greeting.

'It's a pleasure to meet you, Ms Marston.'

That 'pleasure' was laced with a darkly sardonic intonation that turned it into a mockery of the true meaning of the word.

And it made Skye recall, so unwillingly, the way that earlier he had taunted her, 'Do we shake hands formally and really do everything totally back to front?'

The memory almost made her snatch her hand away, jumping back from the burn of his skin against hers, the pressure of palm on palm. But to do that was to risk alerting his father to the fact that something was wrong. At the moment, Cyril Antonakos was beaming with proud satisfaction as he watched what he believed was the first meeting between his fiancée and the estranged son who had newly returned home. How quickly that smile would fade, his mood changing rapidly if he was even to suspect that they had met before—never mind realising in what circumstances that meeting had taken place.

Just thinking of it made Skye's hand shudder still within Theo's grasp, and feeling it he tightened his grip on her cruelly. Looking into the black depths of his eyes, she saw the danger that smouldered there, searing over her face in a look of pure contempt. It was as if he was sending her a wordless message through the merciless pressure on her fingers.

'I can break you as quickly and easily as I can crush your hand,' he seemed to be saying. 'And I will—as and when I want to.'

She had been waiting for him to act ever since. All through the painfully awkward moments after Cyril's arrival, and Theo's realisation of just what her position in his family was. Then she had had to go to her room to shower and change, and get ready for the evening. She had had to leave father and son alone then, unable to find any excuse to stay with them, but she had rushed through her preparations, terrified by the thought that when she returned to the main living room Theo might have decided to tell his father the truth, and all hell would have broken loose.

She had nerved herself to see a dark scowl on the older man's face. A smug, cruel satisfaction lighting his son's black eyes. Struggling with the fear that gripped her at the thought that she might be told to pack her bags and go home—and that her father, her family, could rot in hell—she had found that her legs were trembling so hard they would barely support her as she'd made her way from her bedroom on the lower floor and into the airy white-painted living room.

But Theo had said nothing, it seemed. If he had then Cyril would not have come forward with a smile to give her his usual peck on the cheek, and offer her a drink.

'We're having champagne tonight, my dear,' he said. 'It is, after all, a time for celebration.'

'The return of the prodigal son,' Theo supplied dryly.

Like his father, he got up from his seat as she came into the room and was holding out to her a delicate crystal flute filled with bubbling pale wine.

'And of course to celebrate your own arrival into the family.'

He was so close to her that there was no way his father could have seen the cold black stare that accompanied the apparently welcoming words. But Skye saw it, and as a result her hand shook so violently as she took her drink that some of the champagne slopped over the edge and spilled onto the fine silk of her skirt.

'Careful,' Theo said. 'You don't want to spoil things.'

He smiled as he spoke, but the icy glitter of his eyes, and the soft but deadly menace of his tone, left Skye in no doubt at all that the warning was meant in a way that was very different from a concern about her dress.

As a result she had been desperately on edge all evening, waiting for the axe to fall, for Theo to speak out and reveal the dark secret that would ruin everything.

But for now he was clearly biding his time, and hiding his cruel intent behind a smiling mask.

'So how did you two meet?' he asked now, pushing aside his plate and leaning back in his chair, a glass of rich red wine in one hand.

It was an innocent enough question—on the surface at least. But underneath the lazily drawled words lurked so many dangerous rocks that could sink her totally if she wasn't careful.

Instinctively Skye turned to Cyril, conceding to him automatically. When he had come up with his proposal, he had insisted on absolute secrecy. Their marriage was to look genuine, with no hint of the deal behind it, and of course both Skye and her father had been only too glad to agree.

'Business,' was what he said, helping himself to another portion of the rich baklava that had formed their dessert. 'Skye's father runs a couple of my hotels in England.'

'In London?' Both Theo's tone and his eyes had sharpened and Skye shivered faintly, knowing where his thoughts were heading.

'No—Suffolk. Country house hotels—part of the group but out of the capital.'

'But Suffolk isn't far from London, is it?'

Theo raised his glass to his lips, sipped slowly, black eyes moving to lock with grey over the top of it. His fierce, unwavering gaze held hers mesmerically.

'Do you go into London very often, *Kyria* Marston?'

'Skye, please.'

She forced it from between lips that felt as if they were carved from wood.

'And, no—I don't go into London.'

'Not at all?'

Careful! Skye warned herself. One false step and he would swoop like that hunting eagle. But she didn't want him to think he had her on the run. It might feel like that, of course—she was very definitely trapped with her back against a wall, but she was damned if she was going to run away in panic and leave the field to him. She might just as well surrender right here and now and tell Cyril the truth about their meeting herself.

She could at least give Theo Antonakos a run for his money.

Deliberately she picked up her own glass, swirled the wine around in the bottom of it, then looked him straight in the eye again.

'Well, obviously, I do go to London every now and then—but not often. And to tell you the truth, I can't remember the last time I was there.'

Her defiance caught his attention. One black brow lifted sharply in sardonic response and he inclined his dark head in a small acknowledgement of the way she had parried his attack.

Oh, but she was good, Theo admitted to himself. This Skye Marston was a superb actress—so good that, if he didn't now know exactly what was going on, he would have been totally convinced by her performance.

He had met her precisely twice—for less than a day at a time—and on those occasions she had been perhaps half a dozen different women, changing her personality and her behaviour as quickly and easily as he changed his clothes.

Looking at her now, no one would ever guess that she had been that nervous, distressed creature in the London bar, let alone the wild, passionate woman who had been in his bed that night.

Now here she was the picture of cool elegance in that sleek turquoise silk dress, sleeveless and with a deep vee neckline. Silver glittered at her ears and around the long graceful neck, exposed by the way she had piled that glorious rich coloured hair up at the back of her neck, and she looked calm, relaxed and totally in control.

But she couldn't really be in control, any more than he could. She had to know that their shared secret was there, between them, like a dark shadow.

He lifted his glass again to drink, then reconsidered and only pretended to sip from it. His head was clouded enough. His thoughts had been reeling since the instant in which his father's announcement had hit him like a punch to his jaw, and he still hadn't decided what to do about it.

'You don't want to go out—to clubs—or bars?'

He wasn't quite sure who was watching whom—only that it seemed to him as if there were no one in the room but the two of them. His father might have disappeared completely, and the quiet, decorous presence of a couple of maids barely impinged on his consciousness.

'Skye doesn't frequent clubs and such.'

It was Cyril who answered, reminding Theo sharply of the fact that he was there, at the head of the table. That this was his house—his father's home—and the woman opposite was his father's future bride.

'That's one of the things that attracted me to her. Her innocence. She's not like so many modern young women.'

This time Theo really did have to gulp down a large mouthful of his wine, if only to stop himself from laughing out loud, or making some cynical comment, revealing just precisely how he felt about that statement.

So she had his father totally conned. The old man had no idea at all what she was really like.

So why didn't he just tell him? Why didn't he just open his mouth and say the words?

Your fiancée is not at all the woman you think she is.

The words sounded so clearly inside his head that for one heart-stopping moment he almost thought he'd said them aloud and froze, waiting for the explosion that would follow.

But nothing happened. The declaration had just been in his imagination and the conversation continued just as before—his father blithely ignorant of the emotional grenade that had almost exploded right in his face.

Because that was the effect it would have had. In one

split second, Cyril Antonakos would have gone from being the proudly possessive fiancé of a beautiful, stylish, sexy…

Oh, *Theos,* so devastatingly sexy…

A gorgeous, glamorous, much younger woman.

One moment, Cyril would have been the envy of all men with such a woman on his arm—the next he would have known the sordid truth.

'Her mother has been unwell. So Skye spends most of her time at home, caring for her.'

Except when she's out trawling bars, picking up strange men…

Once more Theo had to bite down hard on his lower lip to stop the words from escaping.

Skye's stunning eyes had dropped, staring down at her hands on the table, and it was all he could do not to laugh out loud in cynical admiration. As a pose of innocent modesty, it was damn near perfect—except that he knew it was a lie and so did she.

So why didn't he just admit it? Why didn't he announce to his father that the woman Cyril thought was a sweet, unworldly, family type wasn't anything of the sort?

Because if he did then, as well as damning her, he would destroy himself in his father's eyes. In fact, he would probably end up painted as the villain of the piece and Cyril would turn his back on him once and for all—for good this time. His father would cut him out of his life without a second thought.

And he had vowed that if his father ever held out an olive branch of peace he would grab it with both hands. That he would do everything in his power to repair the breach that had come between them; end the estrangement if he possibly could.

That was why he was here now. Why he had come to be the best man at the wedding—unaware of just who the bride his father had chosen was. He knew what interpretation his father would probably put on it. That he had come crawling back because he thought that doing so would change Cyril's mind about cutting him out of his will.

Well, if that was the case, then he would take a great delight in letting the old man know that he had no need at all of anyone else's money. He had more than enough of his own.

But this island was a very different matter. Helikos had come to Cyril through his first wife—Theo's mother. It had been in her family for centuries. Calista Antonakos had been buried here, as had both her father and mother before her. It was Theo's rightful inheritance, and one he would fight for with the last strength in his body. He certainly didn't intend to lose it because of some little gold-digger who had caught his father's attention. This year's wife who, if she followed the example of every other *Kyria* Antonakos, would be here and gone again in the space of a couple of years.

'That is unusual,' he managed, knowing from the tiny flicker of a glance in his direction that Skye was unable to control that the acid tone of the words hadn't been lost on her. 'I have to admit that in anyone else I might find it hard to accept about any modern young woman. But, having met your lovely fiancée, I can believe anything of her. Why, when I first encountered her this afternoon, she was embarrassed at being caught in just her swimming costume— in spite of the fact that it was a far more modest design than so many I have seen.'

She was listening hard again. All her attention was focused on his face, and the way those slender, elegant hands were nervously folding her napkin over and over on itself betrayed the inner tension that she had managed to smooth from her expression. She was not at all sure just in what direction he was going to take this and that thought gave him an intense, dark satisfaction.

He waited a nicely calculated moment before continuing with deliberate casualness.

'In fact, there was one woman I met last weekend… She was exactly Skye's age—and build—but the skirt she wore was barely there. She was probably showing far more flesh than you were this afternoon, Stepmama.'

Oh, she didn't like that! She had definitely winced at that 'Stepmama', flinching back in her chair at his tone.

'So it was hardly surprising that she got herself into trouble with some roughs in a bar—'

But Skye had clearly had enough. Dropping the napkin down on the table, she suddenly met his mocking gaze head on, a new flame of bravado in her soft grey eyes.

'That's precisely why I never go into bars or clubs if I can help it!' she declared defiantly. 'You can never tell what sort of thug you might meet there.'

Thug! It was meant to sting and it did.

Whatever else he had been that night, *thug* didn't describe it. He had treated her as well as she had any right to expect, when she had come on to him as she had. But of course she would want to make out that she had been the innocent in all this, to win the sympathy vote, just in case Cyril ever found out the truth.

A black tide of rage swamped his mind, drowning all rational thought, and his hand clenched so tightly on the stem of the wineglass that he was within an inch of snapping it sharply in two.

He couldn't stand to be in the room with the lying, conniving little bitch any longer. He had to get out of here or explode. And if he did lose his temper, then he would take Skye Marston and her calculated play-acting with him. He would tell the truth about their meeting—give his father every single gory detail, and then walk out while the shock waves were reverberating round the house.

But those shock waves would damage his world too.

They would take the fragile peace he had made with his father and shatter it irrevocably into tiny, irreparable pieces. If he took Skye Marston down, then she would take his last chance of inheriting Helikos with her. And he wasn't prepared to let that go.

Not for a cheap little tramp who was clearly well practised in lying through her teeth.

'Well, you don't need to worry about getting rid of me,' he said, tossing down his own napkin and getting to his feet. He directed what he hoped was obviously a fake smile of understanding, his gaze going to where his father's hand still rested on her arm.

'I can see that you two would obviously like to be alone—and I'd hate to intrude. Besides, I'm expecting a call from a young lady.'

It was only his secretary with news of a contract he was working on, but hell would freeze over before he would admit to that.

'So I'll say goodnight, Father—Stepmama. And I'll see you in the morning.'

He was proud of the way that he managed to stroll from the room. Pleased with the fact that he didn't pause or look back, or even show that he gave a damn about what he was leaving behind him. He knew he appeared relaxed, casual and totally at ease.

The truth couldn't be more different.

Because, no matter how much he might tell himself that he had kept quiet only because of Helikos, he knew that the real truth was much more complicated than that. Ever since that night they had spent together in London he hadn't been able to get the searingly erotic images of Skye Marston out of his thoughts—and he still couldn't. Just sitting opposite her had set off a string of heated images that circled over and over in his thoughts until he felt he would go mad.

He didn't want to think of them—didn't want to think of her.

But the truth was that he could think of nothing else.

CHAPTER SEVEN

HE MIGHT as well face facts; he was never going to sleep.

Theo finally admitted to himself that he had no chance at all of drifting into the welcome unconsciousness of slumber, no matter how hard he tried.

He had been tossing and turning in his bed for an hour or more now, and even working on the intensely boring business documents he had tried to use to numb his mind into sleeping had not had the desired effect. He was as wide awake as he had been when he'd left the dining table—wider, in fact, as his struggle not to think of Skye Marston had left him feeling more and more restless with each second that passed.

Eventually he gave up completely, tossed the file down onto the floor, flung himself out of bed and dragged on the pair of swimming shorts that he had discarded earlier.

He had wanted to swim earlier and had been frustrated. Finding Skye in the pool had driven every other thought from his head.

But now he felt so restless and edgy, with a tension building up inside him like the growing oppression before a storm. He had to act or explode. He had to do *something*! And exercise was the sanest, the safest thing he could think of.

Swimming in the still of the night, with only the moon for light, was a calming, relaxing experience. There was no one around, only the sound of an owl hooting once or twice to disturb the silence. Theo swam the length of the pool over and over and over again, backwards and forwards. Long, powerful strokes swept through the water, his muscular legs kicked again and again, until at last he felt a degree of peace descend on him.

Slowly, he began to tire, but still he pushed himself harder and further until his muscles ached and his breathing had a raw edge to it.

'Enough,' he muttered at one last turn. 'Enough.'

Now, at last, he felt he might sleep.

If he could just keep Skye Marston from his mind then he might actually get some rest. It was after one in the morning, time to go to bed.

The single-storeyed pool house was in darkness. Only a small lamp by the door glowed to break up the pitch-black that came from being so far out in the country without a single street lamp for miles. But Theo knew his way around from growing up here as a boy. Shaking the water drops from his soaked hair, he padded into the hall, confident and sure on bare feet. Pausing only to snatch up a towel from a hook in the shower room, he made his way to the kitchen, rubbing himself dry as he went.

The light switch was to his left. Not even needing to look, he reached out a hand and clicked it on.

And froze in shock at the sight of the silent female figure sitting at the kitchen table, her face pale, her back stiffly upright, and her hands folded on the surface in front of her.

She was dressed in just a simple white tee shirt and jeans, her feet bare. The long red hair was loose and fell unstyled over her shoulders and down her back; there was no trace of make-up at all that he could see on her pale, soft face, and she looked stunning.

So stunning that he cursed the kick his heart gave just at the sight of her. The next moment he instinctively moved the towel he was holding so that it fell down in front of him, hiding the instant hardness that strained against the front of his shorts. How could he still respond to just the sight of this woman like this when he now knew just what she was?

An hour's swim in the cool water of the swimming pool and he still felt like this! Hot and hungry in the space of a heartbeat. He was frankly surprised that the remains of the water on his body weren't evaporating from the heat of his skin in a cloud of steam. What he needed was to go and plunge back into the water.

That or a very long, very cold shower.

'What the hell are you doing here?'

'Waiting for you,' Skye said quietly. 'We have to talk.'

'No, we don't. I don't have to do anything I don't want and I don't want to talk to you.'

Skye drew in a deep breath and carefully tried to adjust her thoughts, find the new approach that would fit better with this obviously truculent mood he was in.

'I need to talk to you.'

'Maybe you do—though I don't see why. Seems to me you made your decision about things a week ago when you decided to use me for a one-night stand and then disappear out of my life—back to my father's bed.'

'Oh, no!'

That brought her head up sharply. She couldn't have him believing that! The situation was bad enough as it was, but she couldn't let him continue to think that way.

'I never—I mean—we never... We don't share a bed, your father and I. And we've never...'

Her voice trailed off as Theo slashed a hand through the air in a brutal silencing gesture.

'Enough!' he declared harshly. 'Way too much information. Though at least I'm spared the worry that my papa might start banging on the door, demanding to be let in, having woken in the middle of the night and found that his fiancée has crept away from his bed for a midnight assignation with his son.'

There was such savage anger in the last words that Skye
found herself flinching back in her chair, fearful of the cold
fury in his voice. But Theo made no move towards her. In
fact, from the moment that he had come in the door and
found her sitting here, he hadn't moved an inch. Instead he
was standing stock still, just as he had when he'd flicked
on the light to see her.

'N-no—that won't happen.'

The shake in her voice didn't come from the moment of
fear. Instead, it was all purely feminine awareness. She desperately needed to get her thoughts and her feelings under
control so that she could function properly. But functioning
at all was almost beyond her; functioning *properly* was entirely out of the question. And it became more difficult with
every second that passed simply because of the way that
Theo looked.

She knew he'd been swimming because she'd heard the
faint splashing of the water as she'd made her way up from
the lower level where her bedroom was to the main terrace.
She hadn't dared to use the lift inside the house in case
Cyril woke and heard its faint hum and came to see what
was going on, so she had used the outdoor stairs that were
carved into the rock of the cliffside, moving hesitantly in
the dimly lit darkness.

The moon had been shining down on the swimming pool
as she'd passed it, keeping closely to the shadows so as not
to be seen. And in the pale light she had seen Theo's dark
head, the flash of his muscular arms as he powered through
the water, from one end to the next—a swift, neat turn, and
back again. Again and again.

The moonlight had turned him into an eerie, almost un-
earthly being. His broad chest and back had been bathed
with silver, gleaming and beautiful, making her think of a
dolphin she had seen out in the bay only that morning. She
had stayed there for a few stolen minutes, watching hyp-

notised, unable to turn away. Her mouth had dried and her
heart felt as if it were beating a rapid tattoo in her chest.
She could have stayed there all night, but the sudden fear
of being seen, either by the man in the pool or his father,
had pushed her into action. Fear had sent her hurrying to
the pool house where she had waited, nerves stretched taut
with apprehension, until she had heard Theo come in the
door.

When he'd switched the light on, all the feelings she had
experienced outside had flooded back in full force. But in
a very different way.

Where outside he had been silver and darkness, elemental, ethereal, a fantasy of a merman, here he was heat and
light and physical strength. He was a real man with warm,
bronzed skin, still spattered lightly with sparkling water
drops. His black eyes burned under lush, thick lashes, and
the blood that pulsed through his veins made his body glow
with health and masculine vigour.

The moon man had made her heart catch in admiration
and astonishment, but she had only wanted to watch and
keep her distance from him. This man made her think of
life and passion and sex and her own blood heated at the
memory of how it had felt to be held in his arms, her head
pillowed on the hard, warm width of that chest.

'Your father is fast asleep. I heard him snoring. He had
plenty to drink at dinner.'

'So did I, but it didn't exactly guarantee a night's sleep.'

Theo rubbed the towel over his still wet hair, ruffling it
in a way that Skye found shockingly endearing. He looked
suddenly young and almost boyish in a way that she would
be all kinds of a fool to even think of believing. Theo
Antonakos was no boy—and she would do well to remember that. He was all man—and hard and dangerous with it.

'If it had, you wouldn't have found the house empty
when you arrived.'

He paused, cold black eyes searing over her in sharp assessment.

'Or was that the idea? Did you have plans of sneaking into my bed and seducing—?'

'No!'

She couldn't even let him finish the appalling sentence. Couldn't let him allow even the *thought* of such a thing into his mind.

'No way! That wasn't what I had in mind at all. As I said, I came to talk.'

Theo's sigh was weary, resigned, as he raked a hand through his damp hair and slicked it back from his face.

'Then can it wait until I put some clothes on?'

'Oh—yes—sorry—of course.'

She was gabbling like an idiot, wondering if he had caught her watching him like a child in a sweet shop, almost drooling over the delights on show.

She must *not* think like that. Think practical, Skye. Find something to *do*—to distract you. If she even let in the thought of him stripping off those clinging swimming shorts, rubbing the big body dry...

No!

Such thoughts were far too dangerous to her peace of mind.

What peace of mind? She hadn't known any such thing since *that night,* when Theo Antonakos had come into her life like a nuclear explosion. And now she was struggling to deal with the devastation that was the aftermath.

'Of course. You go and change. Shall I make some coffee?'

'You really do want to make sure that I have no chance at all of sleeping tonight, don't you? No coffee. And no wine. Seems to me I'm going to need a clear head for this. There's some mineral water in the fridge. Glasses in the cupboard above it.'

He had disappeared in the direction of the bedroom by the time that any of his comments really registered on Skye's already jumbled brain.

You really do want to make sure that I have no chance at all of sleeping tonight, don't you?

Had he meant that, like her, he had been lying awake, unable to sleep? Was that why he had taken to swimming in the middle of the night?

And if so, then what sort of thoughts had kept him awake and restless?

Don't go there! she told herself. Don't risk it!

Because the truth was that she didn't know which was the greater risk to her mental balance: knowing that Theo had lain awake thinking of her—or knowing that he had *not*.

She didn't have time to think, anyway. She had barely found the water and the glasses before Theo was back with her.

He had pulled on a loose navy tee shirt and a pair of jogging trousers. Both items were old and baggy and shouldn't have been sexy at all. But it didn't matter what this man wore, he still took her breath away. Perhaps it was because she knew, and remembered so well, just what the body underneath the clothes was like, so that he could have worn an old sack and still have had the impact of a blow to her heart.

She had a nasty little fight with herself to keep her hand from shaking as she filled a glass with the sparkling water and held it out to him. The faint brush of his fingers as he took it from her sent a sensation like an electric shock shooting up her arm and to disguise the betraying reaction she reached for her own glass and gulped down half of it without pausing for breath.

'So talk.' Theo had barely touched his own drink before putting the glass back down on the table. He leaned against

the wall and folded his arms across his chest, narrowed eyes
focusing tightly on her face. 'You said you wanted to talk—
so talk.'

'Are you going to say anything?'

Oh, damn, she hadn't meant it to come out like that.
She'd planned on being calm and reasonable. On coming
round to the point gradually. Instead she'd just blurted out
what was uppermost in her mind without a second's
thought.

'About what?'

'Oh, don't play games! You know very well about what!
Are you going to say anything to your father?'

Theo's dark head went back, resting against the door
post, his black, gleaming stare impenetrable and impassive
in a coldly inscrutable face.

'My father...' he said at last, drawling the words out with
a slow deliberation that tightened nerves already close to
snapping until she felt she wanted to scream. 'Why should
I tell him anything?'

'Oh!'

The unexpected answer was such a relief that all the
tension left Skye in a sudden rush so that she sagged against
the nearest chair like a puppet whose strings had been cut.
The release from tension was so great that her head was
spinning with it and she was totally unable to think of anything beyond the feeling of elation that rushed through her
like a flood tide.

'Oh, thank you!' She gasped. 'Thank you! Thank...'

The words shrivelled on her lips as her vision cleared
and she caught the way he was looking at her. She saw the
dark frown that drew his black brows together, the cold,
assessing glance from those jet eyes, and suddenly knew
she had made a terrible mistake.

'You...'

'*I'm* not going to tell my father anything,' Theo stated icily. 'I think that's your responsibility.'

'What?'

Skye had been swallowing a sip of water as he spoke and she knew a moment of real horror as her throat seemed to close around the drink, threatening to choke her. It was only with a struggle that she managed to regain control, and gulp it down. But even then her voice on the question was shrill and raw, as if her vocal cords were still tightly twisted.

'What do you mean?'

'I know you heard what I said.'

Theo levered himself away from the wall and moved into the adjoining sitting room, flinging himself down into a chair and leaning back, stretching out long legs on the wooden floor in front of him.

'And I'm damn sure you understood it. So why ask for an explanation? You know this is what you have to do.'

'But—yes, of course I understand, but…'

Theo's sigh was a masterpiece—a perfect blend of irritation, impatience and a ruthless control and his eyes were cold as ice floes as he turned them on her.

'You weren't thinking of doing anything else?'

'But I can't!'

Nightmare visions of the disastrous consequences that would follow if she did as Theo expected filled Skye's thoughts, leaving her shaking and fighting back tears.

Her whole world would fall apart. No, there would be no world for her if that was to happen. Her family would be destroyed—her father in prison…her mother…

'I won't do it! I can't!'

'You don't have any alternative,' Theo stated with unyielding brutality. 'Either you tell him or I do.'

Skye closed her eyes against the fear that crawled along her spine. He didn't know what he was asking. But she

couldn't tell him. She had given her word to Cyril that she
would never reveal to anyone the real reason for their marriage, and if she broke it then her father would be in trouble—but her mother would be the one who would suffer.

'Please don't do this,' she whispered. 'Please.'

'So what would you prefer I did?' Theo enquired with
dark cynicism. 'Let my father live a lie—and live one myself by watching him marry you? Dance at your wedding?'

The acid on the words was so savage she felt it would
strip the skin from her bones. She wanted to run—to take
to her heels and flee, never looking back. But the time for
that was long gone; if, indeed, she had ever had a chance.
She only had one hope of salvaging anything for her family
from this; though even that was impossible if Theo carried
out his threat.

'I'm not asking that.'

Putting down her glass with a hand that shook so much
she barely avoided dropping it right onto the wooden floor,
she moved to his side, perching herself on the arm of the
chair and looking deep into his dark, closed face.

'But please don't do this, Theo.'

Something flickered in the blackness of his eyes but,
whatever it was, it was definitely not a sign of any weak-
ening or even any concession.

Instead, he regarded her with his face still set in that cold,
stony expression, rejection of her plea radiating from him
like a force. Talking to him was like banging her head hard
against a rough, unyielding wall. It hurt—and it was clearly
having very little effect.

But she still had to try.

'I'm begging you.'

Impulsively she reached forward, grabbed at both his
hands, holding them in her own, willing him to listen.

'Please, Theo.'

Was this the man who had come to her rescue on that

night in London? The man who had held her so warmly, who had kissed her so gently. The man who had made love to her so passionately and so wonderfully. Could he even be the same man?

But inside he must remember—inside he must surely still feel...

His face was just inches away from hers now. She could feel his breath on her cheek, sense the sudden change in his heart rate under the worn navy cotton of his tee shirt. As she watched she saw him snatch an uneven breath, saw his tongue sneak out and, very briefly, touch the sensual lips that, she suddenly realised, were surprisingly dry.

So he wasn't as armoured against her as she had thought! And she most definitely wasn't immune to him. Sitting this close to him, feeling the warmth of his body, knowing the scent of his skin, she felt the deep, primal hunger beating an erotic pulse through her bloodstream.

And the hunger that he seemed to spark in her just by existing was back, gnawing at her inside, scrambling her thoughts into chaos...

'*Theos! Ochi!* Damn you to hell—*ochi! No!*'

Hard hands clamped around her arms, bruising as they lifted her, wrenched her away from him. She hadn't realised that she had leaned so close and she was still stumbling mentally through the shocking confusion, not knowing what was happening to her, not understanding, when he stood up abruptly and forcefully.

'What do you think I am?'

It was a savage roar, one that brought her head up fast—only to drop her gaze just as quickly when she saw the black rage that burned in his face. His height and strength were impressive enough when she was able to face him, standing upright, but now, when his full height towered over her, he was awe-inspiring and more than a little terrifying.

'Theo…' she began tentatively, her voice breaking on his name, but she wasn't sure if he even heard her; and the black blaze of his eyes in the strong-boned face shrivelled any other words in her mouth.

'What do you think I am?' he demanded again, low and savage, making her shrink back against the chair, wishing she could become invisible, or disappear. 'I may not have been on the best of terms with my father over the past years—but do you think I would betray him with you?'

'No—no—I never meant…' Skye tried to interject, horrified at the way he had misinterpreted her actions, seeing an attempt at seduction in the way she had been unable to hide her feelings. But he ignored her in his rage and swept on heedlessly.

'How low do you think I would stoop? How far would you lower yourself to get what you want?'

'I never—'

'No?'

A violent, angry gesture dismissed her weak attempt at a protest, almost as if he were throwing her words right out the window.

'Then what the hell was all that? "Oh, please, Theo… please…"'

Skye could only blink in stunned horror as he suddenly switched to a frighteningly near-accurate copy of her own words, her own voice, and to her shock and distress she caught the note of husky seduction mixed in with the pleading she had aimed for.

'"I'm begging you, Theo…" Oh, yes—you were begging, all right!'

To her total astonishment he suddenly came forward and held out a hand, clearly intending to help her up. Stunned and bemused, Skye could only take the hand he offered, finding herself wrenched to her feet with a force that almost had her flying to the opposite side of the room.

But Theo caught her, whirled her round back to face him, yanked her close. For a long, long moment he simply stared into her face, but then he reached out his free hand, tracing the side of her face, the contours of her cheek, before he pushed his long, powerful fingers into the fall of her burnished red hair.

'Oh, I know what you were begging for. What you wanted was this…'

The kiss he dragged her into was hard and rough, cruelly punishing, devastating. It was meant to tell her exactly what he thought of her and it did. It humiliated, angered, shattered her. And it left her shaking in her shoes at just the thought of what was in his mind.

But then just as suddenly that kiss stopped.

It stopped and Theo lifted his head for a moment, drew in a raw, ragged breath. Molten jet eyes blazed down into hers, searing right through to her soul.

'Oh, yes, my sweet,' he murmured, soft as a deadly snake. '*That's* what you want. What you respond to. What you use to try to entice me into doing as you want.'

'It wasn't like that…' Skye tried to whisper, but her tongue seemed to have frozen in her mouth, unable to speak a word, and he either didn't hear her or ignored her attempt and pushed straight on.

'And do you know what I hate—what I despise the most? It's that even now, when I know that everything you are is a lie, that the woman I met, the woman I slept with, was as false as she could be, that she was promised to someone else—to my own father!—you still can't stop! You still think that you can seduce me round to your way of thinking—to doing what you want me to do. That by offering me your body—'

'No!'

'Yes,' Theo returned harshly. 'Oh, yes. But it won't work, *agape mou*. You don't catch me that way again. I may have been duped at our first meeting—but I don't put my head into the noose a second time. Not for anyone—and certainly not for a conniving, scheming little tramp like you've proved yourself to be.'

'No...' It was all she could manage; all she could think of to say.

But even as she spoke she knew that it was all pointless, that she might just as well have saved herself the effort. Theo wasn't going to listen to her, and, even if he did, there was no way she could refute the appalling accusations he was throwing at her, not unless she offered him some alternative explanation.

And the only explanation she could offer was the truth. A truth that she was forbidden to tell anyone, that she had sworn to keep to herself. If she let it out, she would ruin so many other lives.

While keeping silent only ruined her own.

'No?' Theo scorned. 'Well, I'm sorry, my angel, but I just don't believe you.'

His hand came out, slowly, carefully, so that she didn't have time to react or flinch away.

With the back of one long finger he traced the line of her face, from her temple, down her cheek, along the curve of her jaw. Just for a second, his touch lingered on her mouth, stroking softly, and even though she knew it was impossible, that she was just deceiving herself, in that second, despairingly, Skye would have sworn that the bleak black eyes had been touched with a tiny gleam of regret.

But she had to have been imagining things because the next moment he snatched his hand away, shaking it faintly as if to remove the contamination of her touch. Whatever had been in his eyes vanished completely as his face closed up, harsh and severe, in total rejection of her.

'You have three days,' he told her, each word cold and clear and totally obdurate. 'Three days in which to tell my father the truth. And at the end of that time, if you still haven't told him—then I promise you I will.'

CHAPTER EIGHT

THREE days.

It hadn't sounded long when Theo had given Skye the ultimatum. In fact it hadn't sounded like any time at all.

Three days—just seventy-two hours—in which to find the courage to face Cyril and admit to him what had happened. She didn't know how she could do it. She only knew that somehow—God knew how—she *had* to.

But that had been the day before yesterday. Now more than forty-eight hours of the seventy-two had passed—gone. And she was no nearer to bringing herself to do as Theo had ordered.

If anything, she was further away from it than she had ever been.

For one thing, Cyril hadn't even been in the house most of the time. He had spent a large amount of yesterday in the village and had returned in such a dreadful mood that Skye had hurriedly retired to her room and left him to himself. This morning he had ordered the helicopter to take him to Athens at what seemed like the crack of dawn and hadn't been seen since.

Skye could only be thankful that Theo too had made himself scarce. The thought of facing him and the inevitable reaction when he discovered that she still hadn't given in to his demands and told his father the truth made her shiver in genuine fear.

The future seemed dark and bleak, without a single glimmer of hope on the horizon, and she had no idea which way to turn.

If she didn't tell Cyril, then Theo would. But how could

she tell Cyril when doing so would inevitably mean that he would call off the whole engagement and the wedding that was supposed to follow it?

And without that wedding, then her father had no chance of avoiding arrest, because if thwarted then Cyril would surely press charges even more vehemently. And if he was arrested, then her mother...

'Oh, heaven help me!'

Skye sank down onto the nearest chair and buried her face in her hands, giving in to despair.

She had never felt so lost and alone. So totally abandoned by everyone.

'Is there a problem?'

She recognised the husky male voice immediately. It was the one that had haunted her dreams, sounded in her head all day long ever since she had heard it issuing the brutal ultimatum that threatened to shatter her life, and that of all the people she loved.

'Oh, no, there's no problem!' she flung at him, her head coming up sharply, auburn hair tossed back over her shoulder, grey eyes blazing defiance. 'No problem at all! Only the fact that my life finally seemed to be back on some sort of track—one that I could at least cope with. But then I had the misfortune to meet you and now everything's blown up in my face!'

'You haven't told him.' It was a statement, not a question, but Skye still felt he was waiting for a response to it.

'No, I haven't told him!'

If he'd been around in the house, he would have known that. But for his own private reasons Theo had made himself scarce for the past couple of days. Having delivered his ultimatum, he had backed off and left her alone with his father.

Of course, she knew why. He was expecting her to use the time to tell Cyril everything. She supposed that he thought he was being fair—even considerate—by giving her the space and the quiet in which to broach the subject.

Well, he might not have been actually putting pressure on her directly with his words and his presence, but the knowledge that he was there, waiting, watching, like some cruel hunter lurking in the shadows, waiting to pounce if she didn't do as he ordered, had kept her in a permanent state of shivering terror, never knowing when his dark patience would run out and he would move in for the kill.

'For one thing, I haven't had an opportunity, and for another—well, I just don't know how he's going to react.'

'That's something you should have considered before you leapt into bed with a complete stranger.'

The cynicism in Theo's tone seemed all the worse when Skye admitted to herself just how wonderful he looked. With the afternoon sunlight shining on the glossy black hair, making the dark eyes gleam spectacularly between their frame of thick, lush lashes, he was a Greek god come to life in modern dress. The long, lean legs were clothed in jeans so tight they were positively indecent, and the power of his chest and shoulders was emphasised by the loving cling of the soft tee shirt to the muscled contours. The white material threw the colour of his bronzed skin into sharp relief, his tan already deepened by several days in the Greek sun, and the whole picture was one that made her mouth dry in purely sensual delight.

'I had no idea that the complete stranger was going to turn out to be my fiancé's son!'

'No, I don't suppose you did,' Theo drawled, strolling into the room and dropping down into a chair opposite with indolent ease. 'That was rather unfortunate for you.'

'Unfortunate!' Skye echoed sourly. 'That has to be the understatement of the year!'

'But would it have made things any more justifiable if I'd been a perfect stranger? You would still have been unfaithful to the man you were engaged to. Or are you one of those people who believe that the crime is not in the actual action, but in getting found out?'

'Not at all!' Skye denied his words furiously 'I don't expect you to believe me, but I don't make a habit of indulging in one-night stands with complete strangers!'

'You'd be wrong about that—I do believe you.'

'And I wasn't exactly *engaged* to your father at the time—'

The sudden realisation of the words he had inserted quietly into her tirade pulled her up sharp, her head spinning in shock.

She couldn't be hearing properly. Had he said...?

'*What* did you say?' she demanded rawly.

'That I believe you. That you're not the type who makes a habit of indulging in one-night stands with complete strangers.'

'You—you do?'

'Absolutely.'

Stunned relief and delight flooded through her. Her heart leapt, her spirits lifted. A smile she couldn't suppress spread wide across her face.

'That's wonderful! Fantastic! You can't imagine the relief that makes me feel...'

But something was wrong.

Very wrong.

The smile slipped a bit, faded, as she realised that there was no answering lightening of Theo's expression. Instead, his features remained set in the sombre, unyielding cast that they had displayed from the moment he had come into the room.

As sudden doubt crept into her mind and took an uncomfortable hold Skye felt her world tilt on its balance, swaying sickeningly.

'You didn't mean it?' she questioned hesitantly.

'Oh, yes, I meant it. I could hardly think otherwise—could I? After all, I am only too aware that there hadn't been any man before me. You were a virgin that night.'

Another statement. A flat, blank-toned question that rocked her back in her seat, making her stare into his dark, shuttered face. Had she failed so completely in her attempt to look and act sophisticated and experienced?

'I—what—you knew?'

The look Theo shot her was dark with cynical mockery. A black humour that wasn't echoed in any lightening of his expression, not even the tiniest hint of a curve to his sensual mouth.

'Oh, yes, I knew. Do you know what that did to me?'

'You're angry about that?'

She couldn't understand his reaction, couldn't understand what was going through his head at all, and the confusion and uncertainty made her too uncomfortable to sit still. Pushing herself to her feet, she prowled about the room, agonisingly conscious of those deep, dark eyes following her every move until she felt like some specimen under a microscope or a caged animal being closely observed by some coldly analytical scientist.

'I don't get it! I don't understand at all! I—I thought it was a deep-seated male fantasy to be some woman's first lover. To be the one who took her virginity…'

But she'd hit quite the wrong note there. In trying for a levity she was far from feeling, her words had had the effect of lighting the blue touch-paper and failing to stand well back while the whole multicoloured explosion roared into life right in her face.

Theo hurled himself to his feet in a movement that was so expressive of barely controlled violence that it had her stumbling back behind a chair for protection. His face was twisted into a savage scowl that added to her sense of fearful apprehension.

'In a sordid one-night stand in a cheap hotel?' he snarled viciously. 'Oh, yeah—some fantasy! Your—a woman's—first time should be something special—something to remember. Not just thrown away!'

He *meant* it! Skye could hardly believe what she was seeing. Theo truly meant this. It was in his eyes, in his voice.

'Can't you see?' she pleaded with him. 'That's why I did it—why I was with you. I didn't want your—my wedding night to be the first. That's why I was there.'

She'd thought she could make things better by explaining, but to judge from the change of expression, the searing burn of those deep-set eyes, she'd only managed the exact opposite.

'To throw it away on any man you met?'

He was taking it exactly the wrong way.

'Not just any man...'

And it had been special, she told him in the privacy of her thoughts, not daring to let on just *how* special that night had been. It was bad enough knowing it herself, but if she admitted to even a tiny part of it then she knew that it would rip her to pieces inside.

'Oh, don't tell me that you met me and instantly knew I was the love of your life,' Theo scorned.

'No—I'm not saying that.'

'I could have been just anyone.'

'No!' *Never.* 'And the hotel wasn't that cheap!'

Oh, why couldn't she stop? It had been obvious from the start that her attempts to pretend that that night hadn't mattered so much had failed painfully. Theo's scowl, the way his black brows were drawn tightly together, the black eyes blazing beneath them were warning enough that she was blundering blindly into a dangerous minefield where at any moment things might blow up in her face. But still she couldn't help herself. Couldn't stop herself from blurting out totally inappropriate remarks that were only making matters worse.

'It was to me!'

The savage declaration made her jump like a startled rabbit. In fact, that was exactly what she felt like as he came towards her—a small, frightened rabbit, transfixed in the beam of a car's headlights, wishing desperately that she could move.

'I did exactly what you wanted. Took you exactly where you asked. "A quiet, decent hotel",' Theo said, and Skye realised that he was quoting her exactly.

'But, of course, I didn't know who you were then. If I had, then I might have…'

Something about the icy glare he turned on her froze the words on her tongue, cutting them off completely. In dawning horror, she realised just what she was saying, the impression she was giving. A hot tide of red swept right across her face and her hands crept up to cover her mouth, trying to hold the dreadful words back.

But of course it was far too late.

'If you'd known who I was then what, Skye?' Theo pounced on the foolish sentence. 'Would you have held out for more, is that it, hmm? Would you have insisted on a five-star place, or asked for more? Traded your virginity for a night in a penthouse suite, perhaps—or a little room service?'

'I didn't ask for anything from you!'

'Only a night of meaningless sex with an anonymous man.'

'Yes! Yes, that was exactly what I was looking for!'

Skye winced inside at the way that sounded. But she was beyond controlling her voice. Because the truth was that Theo was not reacting in any way as she had anticipated.

Not that she had ever *anticipated* meeting up with the man with whom she had spent that crazy night in London ever again! She had thought that her one night of breaking out into the freedom that soon would be lost to her for ever would be her secret, and hers alone. That it would be totally anonymous, and no one would know.

But there were two problems with that. One was that in no way at all could the sex have been described as 'meaningless'. It had been wild; it had been wonderful. It had pitched her straight from blind innocence and ignorance into a world of sensation, of knowing—and of hunger.

It had been special—so very special.

And it had left an indelible mark on her for ever.

But at least she had managed to keep the anonymous part to exactly that. And as a result she had been quite safe. Until she had come here to Helikos and come face to face with a black twist of fate in the form of Theo Antonakos.

'And that was exactly what I got—and what you got as well. It was what you wanted too! Wasn't it?'

Had she actually been hoping for something else? If she had, then the stupid thought was crushed out of her by his swift retort.

'Well, I sure as hell wasn't looking for marriage!'

'So there you are—we both got exactly what we were looking for. So why can't you leave it at that?'

'You know damn well why!' he flung at her. 'Because it can't be left at that!'

'Why not? Surely if we just put it all behind us and move on, then it can all be over and done with.'

For Theo at least.

'That isn't going to work,' Theo muttered, shaking his dark head slowly.

'Why can't it?'

'Because of who we are—who you are.'

'Me?'

'You're my father's fiancée. That's what makes the difference—all the difference in the world.'

'But it doesn't have to,' Skye protested. 'Only if we let it.'

'*Skye!*'

Her name was a violent sound of outraged fury on his tongue and he raked his hands through his hair, pressing them against the bones of his skull in exasperation.

'Can't you see that there is no "if we let it"?'

'I don't know what you mean.'

'We have no choice but to let it!' Theo told her fiercely. 'You are going to marry my father…and…'

'And?' Skye prompted when he fell silent, seeming to hunt for the words.

'*Theos!* Can you not see it? Can you not feel it?'

'F-feel what?' Skye stammered, though she had a terrible feeling that she knew what was in his thoughts. She knew what she had been hiding from for days and the thought of bringing it out into the open terrified her.

'This thing that's between us.'

'There's nothing between us,' Skye put in hastily, terrified to even let the idea into her mind. 'Nothing at all. I don't know what you're talking about!'

Liar! his look said. *You know exactly what I mean. Exactly what there is.*

'There's an atmosphere—almost an electricity that's in the air between us. I can't keep my eyes—my hands—off you!'

She actually turned white at the words. He watched the blood drain from her cheeks, leaving them pallid and ashen.

He knew exactly how she was feeling. He'd tried to deny it himself at first. But then, like a fool, he'd kissed her. He'd kissed her in anger and contempt, but it hadn't stayed that way. Other, more primitive feelings had swept through him like a tidal wave and he'd known just why he couldn't leave the situation that way—why he couldn't leave the island though, God help him, he'd tried!

He still wanted her. Wanted her more than ever. He didn't care if she was a gold-digger, didn't care about anything but having her back in his bed again.

But she was promised to his father. And he had never taken another man's woman in his life. He didn't intend to start now.

But if she were to leave Cyril...

'It isn't over between us and you know it.'

'It is!' It was a cry of panic, of desperation. 'It is over! It has to be—I'm marrying your father!'

'Then don't!'

There, it was out. Theo told himself. The thing that had been preying on his thoughts all day, every day since the moment he had realised just who she was and why she was here on Helikos. The words that he had been trying not to say, words he had sworn that he would never say, but even as he had done so he had known that he would inevitably one day. He would have to.

For days he'd fought with himself. Fought to stay away from her. Fought the need to be with her. He had set himself to a gruelling regime of exercise, running on the seashore, swimming endless laps of the pool, lifting weights in the small gym his father had had built but had very obviously never used. It had kept him out of her way and it had exhausted his body, but his mind had stayed wide awake.

And at night, in the darkness, the memories had come.

Heated memories of the night they had spent together. The one night when he had known all the sweetness and the passion that her glorious body could offer.

And he had known he wanted more.

The sweetness he wanted to taste all over again. The passion he longed to sate himself on once more.

He had barely managed to cope with the past two days as it was. He had only kept himself from giving in to the magnetic pull her body had for his by telling himself over and over again that she wasn't available, that she was engaged—to his *father,* for God's sake!

She was not only not available, she was forbidden!

But even knowing that, he had endured two nights without sleep. Spent two long days fighting the need to see her. Fighting his body's need to bury himself in her again.

He knew now that that was why he had been so insistent that she tell his father about the night they had spent together. He didn't just want the truth out in the open; he wanted her free from this impossible engagement.

He wanted her all to himself. And he felt he would go mad if he didn't have her.

'Don't marry my father. You can't marry him feeling the way you do about—'

'About you?' Skye inserted swiftly, jerkily. 'I don't feel anything for you!'

'But you do.' Theo dismissed her protest with a contemptuous flick of his hand. 'You feel just the way I do— I can see it in your face. In your eyes whenever I'm near.'

'You arrogant...'

The negligent shrug of broad shoulders under the white tee shirt showed how little he cared about her accusation.

'I may be arrogant, but at least I'm honest.'

Deliberately he took a slow step forward, then another, his eyes fixed on her face, watching every flicker of reaction that she was unable to hide. He saw the way her head went back, the sudden change in her breathing, the darkness of her eyes.

'See?' was all he said, but he knew she'd got the message. Ruthlessly he pressed home his advantage. 'Damn you, Skye, think about this—about what will happen when my father finds out...'

'Why should he find out?'

Her voice had changed again and there was a note in it

now that he couldn't even begin to read. He didn't know
what to feel either. His emotions seemed to be running on
a loop of anger, through concern, exasperation, and an ir-
rational, overwhelming desire to grab her, haul her into his
arms and kiss her senseless. Kissing seemed to be the only
function of that soft, sexy mouth that was simple, uncom-
plicated—and totally understandable.

Oh, who was he trying to kid? Kissing her might start
out as the most straightforward thing in this whole tangle
of knots that simply being with Skye tied him up in, but it
would very rapidly turn into the most complex and prob-
lematical situation before he had time to breathe. He
couldn't kiss Skye while she was with his father; and, for
her own personal, private reasons, she seemed determined
to try to hold fast to this appalling engagement.

'I can't believe you're asking me that question.'

'I could pretend—'

'Oh, hell, yes, you could!'

Theo couldn't hold back the cynical laughter that escaped him at the thought.

'You could pretend, all right—but if you wanted to be
convincing you'd have to turn in a performance that's a
damn sight better than the one you're giving me!'

He'd actually silenced her. For the first time since he'd
come into the room and found her sitting on the chair with
her head in her hands, she was finally stunned into silence,
staring up at him, her face frozen in shock.

'There's something else, isn't there? Something you're
not telling me. Damnation, Skye, just what is going on
here?'

Her eyes flinched away from his, dropping down to stare
at the carpet with an impossibly fierce concentration.

'I don't know what you mean.'

'Don't give me that!'

Dropping to one knee in front of her, he caught her chin

in his hand, pushing it up so that she was forced to meet his gaze. When she tried to pull away he simply clamped his fingers more tightly around her jaw and drew her back inexorably to face him.

'Tell me!' he commanded. 'I want to know just why you are so determined to marry my father.'

CHAPTER NINE

How could she ever answer that? Skye asked herself. She was trapped, no matter which way she turned. Tied by so many different promises to so many people, and knowing she had no way out. There was the promise she had made to her father—others to Cyril...

But the one promise that truly mattered to her was the one that she had made in her heart to her mother. Claire Marston knew nothing of the real reasons why her daughter was suddenly going to marry a much older Greek millionaire; she would have been horrified if she did. But in her heart Skye had promised that she would do anything—everything—she could to ensure that her mother had the health and strength to enjoy as much of life as she could. And if that meant giving up some of her own life, her own happiness, in return, then she believed it was worth it.

So now she had only one choice open to her, one path she could possibly follow.

And she took it.

'Why?' she echoed with what she hoped was a deceptively lightweight and flippant air. She had started on this coldly casual act to protect herself; she couldn't afford to let it slip now. 'Isn't it obvious? Because he asked me.'

Once again, Theo's response surprised her. She had expected anger. She had expected contempt. She had expected that he would simply toss her aside—mentally at least— and just walk out. So she was stunned when he shook his head in total rejection of what she was saying.

'Not good enough,' he stated with a cold finality.

His absolute calmness was somehow more disturbing

than if he had lost his temper and shouted at her. A sudden, scary feeling that she was fighting for her life pushed her towards an even more outrageous declaration.

'You don't think that's good enough? Why ever not?'

Her pause was supposed to give him time to respond, but he didn't take it. Instead, he seemed to be waiting for her to speak again.

But what could she say? If he only knew it, she had spoken the exact truth when she had given him her answer. Cyril had offered marriage as a way out of the appalling problems that beset her family, and, in despair, with no way to turn, she had accepted him.

'What's so difficult to believe about it?' she demanded, the anguish in her heart putting a sharpness on her tongue that she couldn't have managed if she'd planned it. 'Who in their right mind would want to turn down this?' She waved a hand in an all-encompassing gesture that took in the whole room, the patio out beyond the doors, and the blue water of the swimming pool beyond that. 'I certainly wasn't going to.'

It was only when his face changed, his expression hardening, eyes turning to black flint, that she realised how a moment before he had had an entirely different look. She had been near to some sympathy, some understanding from him, and now he had backed away again. Physically as well as mentally.

He had moved back from her; his grip on her jaw loosening. The barriers were up between them once more and it hurt so badly that she had to blink back tears.

But it was better this way.

Safer.

The implications of that word, 'safer', were ones she flinched away from admitting to herself. They gave her an idea, though. If she tried to defend herself from Theo's questions, then she very rapidly found herself with her back against the wall. It was time to stand up for herself—go on the attack instead.

Wrenching her chin free from his loosened grasp, she tried to push Theo aside, get to her feet. But the barrier of his big body offered far more resistance than she had ever imagined. Her push had no effect whatsoever on him, but it made her fingers curl in shock at the sensations that fizzed up her nerves as they encountered the heat and hardness of his powerful chest.

Giving up the attempt to make him move, she scrambled inelegantly off the chair over its arm, turning hastily to confront him while she had the advantage of height because he still knelt on the floor.

'Why does it matter so much to you what happens between me and your father? I understood that you and he weren't exactly close.'

She'd got under his guard with that one. She saw it register in the depths of his eyes and knew a shiver of apprehension as his jaw tightened and a muscle in his cheek tugged sharply.

'Who told you that?'

'Your father, of course.'

Her throat dried as Theo uncoiled his long body and slowly stood up. Perhaps it was the fact that she had no shoes on and in bare feet was inches smaller, but Skye felt that never before had he seemed so tall, so imposing, so *big* as when he towered over her now. Her toes curled on the polished wooden floor as she fought against the craven impulse to turn and run.

'And what did he tell you about it?'

'That—that you had a disagreement.'

'Which is something of an understatement.'

The bitter irony of Theo's response made it plain that it had been anything but a 'disagreement'.

'What was it about?'

'Do you really want to know?' Theo demanded sharply. 'Really?'

'Yes, I do.' Skye tried to sound much more certain than she actually felt. 'It might make me understand things more.'

Something in Theo's expression warned her that that was a vain hope. But she had taken this path now. She was determined to see it through.

'Tell me,' she said unevenly.

Theo pushed his hands deep into the pockets of his jeans and strolled away towards the open patio doors where he stood, staring out at the clear blue water of the pool glinting in the sun.

'My father disowned me because I wouldn't marry the bride of his choice.'

'What?' Skye was stunned. 'You're kidding!'

Theo swung round to face her again and the deadly serious cast of his stunning features made the half-laughing protest and disbelief fade rapidly from her face.

'Do I look as if I am joking?' he demanded haughtily, his accent sounding very pronounced on the question. 'Believe me, it is not a topic I would be flippant about.'

'But—he—I mean—why?'

Theo's mouth curved into a grim travesty of a smile that had no trace of humour at all in it.

'My father has always tried to run my life,' he said at last. 'When I was small he took control completely—I could barely breathe without his permission. My mother died when I was five—two years later I was sent to boarding-school in England.'

'At seven?'

She looked truly shocked, Theo reflected. Shocked, and something else he couldn't quite interpret. If he'd been caught in a weak moment he might have called it sympathetic, but he would probably be fooling himself to even consider it.

'I wasn't the only one,' he returned dryly. 'I was in a class of boys that age. My father was determined that I should get the best education possible—for him that meant an English public school, then an English university. Then, of course, working with him in the Antonakos Corporation.'

'He had your life all mapped out for you.'

Theo's mouth twisted cynically.

'Right down to the woman I should marry.'

Skye perched on the arm of one of the big chairs. Her eyes still had that strange shadowed look in them. Concentrate on that, he told himself fiercely. At least if he kept his gaze—and his attention—focused on her eyes, then he would stop himself from thinking too much about the rest of her.

About the slide of her hair over the bare, lightly tanned shoulder exposed by the slender straps of her lilac-coloured dress. About the way that sitting on the edge of the chair had pulled the already short skirt up even higher on the slim, elegant legs. About the sway of soft breasts clearly not confined in some restricting contraption of satin and Lycra, but moving with each slight gesture she made.

When she lifted a hand to push through her hair his blood pressure mounted to an alarming degree. And the memory of those legs wrapped around his waist like hot silk as she writhed underneath him threatened his ability to think so badly that he barely heard her next comment and had to force his attention back to the present before he lost track of things completely.

'You didn't like her?'

'You really don't know my father too well, do you? I never saw her—and neither, I believe, did he.'

There was no mistaking the emotion that widened her

eyes now. It was total consternation—mixed with a touch of disbelief.

'You'd never even met her?'

Theo shook his head firmly. 'It was to be an arranged marriage. A cold-blooded financial arrangement between my father and hers.'

'And you had no say in the matter?'

'My father certainly didn't intend that I should. I was twenty-seven—more than old enough to start providing him with grandchildren. He had surveyed all the families with daughters of marriageable age, and Agna's father owned land he wanted. That, together with the fact that she was just nineteen, a virgin, and the family fortune, though no match for the Antonakos wealth, was far from inadequate, made her the perfect choice as far as he was concerned.'

'So this Agna didn't get a choice either?'

'Why should she? She was only a daughter, and as far as two greedy old men were concerned she had one real purpose to serve—to marry well, improve the family fortunes, and bear an heir to the combined estate.'

'Oh, don't! You make her sound like a brood mare!'

Skye's voice broke uncontrollably on the words as a result of the bleak thoughts that flooded her mind. At first she been feeling so uptight that she had almost let his explanation of the rift with his father slip by in a haze of shocked disbelief, without registering the impact it had on her personally. All she had thought of was the way *Theo* had been treated, when she should have looked at what it meant for her.

And what it meant for her was an added brutal twist to the knife in her heart, an added sense of being used.

She was only a daughter, and as far as two greedy old men were concerned she had one purpose to serve—to marry well, improve the family fortunes, and bear an heir to the combined estate.

The words seemed to gather an added sense of bitterness with each repetition inside her head. Theo's father had not managed to get his way, by marrying his son off, so he had done the next best thing by taking a young wife who, in her own words, would have to act as 'a brood mare'.

'Not me, sweetheart,' Theo returned harshly. 'I was the one who turned her down, remember. I had no wish to get married. And I lost my own inheritance as a result.'

'He really disinherited you? Cut you out of his will without a penny?'

'That is what the term usually means. Though that "without a penny" isn't strictly accurate. I'd already formed my own company—one with an income my father couldn't touch. No, the part of my inheritance I really lost was this island.'

'Helikos?'

The grim set to Theo's mouth as he nodded twisted her nerves into even more painful knots.

'It was my mother's and it should have come to me. But anything else—forget it! In the five years since I rebelled against the idea of becoming a married man, I've more than doubled my profits. I expect my personal fortune will match my father's now. So you needn't worry that I lost out on the deal.'

'I never...' Skye began, but she was interrupted by the sound of the telephone shrilling through the room. She glanced in the direction of the sound, but it was more important that Theo should know she hadn't been shocked at his father's treatment of him because of the money he had lost.

'That wasn't what was on my mind!' she continued. 'I—'

Once more the sound of the phone cut into her words.

'Aren't you going to answer that?' Theo asked.

'I'm not sure I should. Your father...'

Cyril had made it plain that she was not to interfere in his life. That she was only to be a decorative wife on his arm and in his bed.

'It will probably be him anyway. And if it isn't—well, the reason you're here is that you will be *Kyria* Antonakos in a matter of weeks. So if you're determined to go through with it, you'd better get a taste for acting as the mistress of the house.'

He made a point of walking away to the open doors again, giving her time and privacy for the call.

It *was* Cyril and what he had to say, the tone he used, made icy footsteps dance up and down her spine. He had never, obviously, treated her with much affection, but now his tone was positively brusque, his need to get away quickly desperately worrying.

Skye was suddenly a prey to a terrible fear that something had gone wrong. Had something happened to make Cyril change his mind so that even the sacrifice she was prepared to make wasn't enough? The thought made her realise just how terribly isolated she was, how alone. But with Theo so close at hand she didn't dare to ask, and Cyril issued his last order and switched off the phone even as she was struggling to find a reply.

When Theo swung round again to face her she was still standing by the table, sharp teeth digging into her lower lip, a frown of concern between her brows.

'Theo will look after you,' Cyril had said, and right at this moment she couldn't even begin to think which was worse—this terrible, dragging sense of loneliness and fear, or the thought of being alone with Theo once more.

'He's staying in Athens tonight,' she said flatly when she saw that Theo was looking at her. 'Not coming back till tomorrow. He—he said you'd look after me.'

She lifted her eyes as she spoke, her dove-grey gaze

locking with his, and Theo wondered sharply just what was going through her mind.

He knew what was going through *his*.

His father was not coming back until tomorrow. Twenty-four hours alone with Skye.

Twenty-four hours alone with temptation. A *night* of temptation.

He said you'd look after me.

Oh, *Theos*! His father had no suspicion at all just how he would like to *look after* this woman, or he wouldn't have left her in his care.

He had already been fighting himself desperately for more than forty-eight hours. Could he manage to keep his feelings on a tight rein for another day, here, on his own in the house with her?

It was not something he wanted to risk.

'I have things I need to do.'

'All right.'

She wouldn't look at him as she spoke, but seemed absorbed in a painting that hung on the far wall, concentrating fiercely on the image of Persephone.

'You'll be all right?'

'I'll be fine.'

It was less certain this time, the words faintly uneven. But she still wouldn't look at him.

Was there a thickness in her voice? And the only time he had ever seen anyone blink that hard it had been because they were blinking back...

'Skye?'

Perversely, now that he had what he wanted, Theo found he was more than reluctant to leave. A faint flicker of a smile touched Skye's mouth as she watched him hesitate. But it was a cynical, disturbingly weary smile. And at last she looked at him, or at least she turned her head in his direction, but her unfocused gaze seemed to go straight over his shoulder, avoiding his eyes.

'What are you trying to do?' she questioned with a rough-edged note to the words, as if her words were unravelling as she spoke. 'Do you want to prove that I can't let you go? That that…electricity that you think is between us will make it impossible to part from you?'

'I'd be a fool to think that,' he said with dark softness, 'when I know only too well that you could walk out without a second thought. You've already done it once.'

'I told you it was just for that night.'

'And I told you I don't do one-night stands.'

This time when she blinked her gaze seemed to come back into focus and her dark, cloudy eyes met his just once, then flinched away again.

'Are you claiming you wanted more?'

'It was certainly an experience that I would have liked to repeat if you hadn't bolted out of there like a frightened rabbit before I even had time to wake up.'

'I did not *bolt*!'

'You sure as hell didn't hang around. What was it, sweet Skye? A sudden realisation that you had a conscience after all?'

'It wasn't that at all.'

Skye aimed for defiance, almost made it, but her voice slipped a little on the last couple of words. But she felt as if she were fighting for her life here and she had no intention of letting him see it.

The acid burn of misery ate into her soul at the memory of the way she had felt when she had left that hotel room. At the time she had thought that nothing could make her feel worse. Now she knew how wrong she had been.

'I said at the time that it was my way or nothing. And you agreed.'

'I went along with what you said,' Theo corrected coldly.

'I don't recall signing any agreement in blood. I was fool enough to think you might wait around at least for breakfast.'

'I told you how it would be. Why should you complain when I stuck to my word?'

'I didn't like the way it made me feel.'

'And that was?'

'Used.'

It was the last thing she had expected and the single word made her thoughts reel in shock.

Used.

He had felt *used*?

How did he think his father had made her feel?

'Join the club!' she flashed back, her spinning brain unable to think of anything less provocative in the few seconds that were at her disposal.

'What?'

For a moment she thought that once more Theo's grasp of English had failed him and that was why he was frowning his lack of comprehension. But the next second she realised how dangerously close she had come to giving away the true details of her situation.

'Well, you have to admit it's unusual for a man to feel that way…' She covered her tracks hastily. 'That's how most women feel when a man only wants a one-night stand. It doesn't do any harm for you to get a taste of your own medicine.'

'I did not *use* you!'

'We both used each other. It was just—what was it you said? A night of meaningless passion.'

'Meaningless is the truth. You couldn't get out of there quick enough!'

Oh, if only he knew the reality of it!

Skye felt tears threaten and fought against them hard,

tightening her jaw and clamping her mouth tight shut against the little cry of distress that almost escaped her.

If only he knew how she had felt that morning when she had woken to find herself curled up close to his long, warm body, clasped tight in the strength of his arms.

For a few, wonderful moments reality hadn't quite sunk in and she had lain there, keeping her eyes closed, a small, ridiculous smile on her face, just enjoying the sensation of being held like this. How she had wished that she could just stay there, held close, and never, ever move again.

And when she had finally left the room, her face had been streaked with tears. Tears of loss for a man who hadn't even known who she was and—if fate was kind—would never know.

But of course fate had not been kind. The truth was that fate had been at its cruellest that night, and again when it had brought her here, to this island just three days ago.

Because it had brought her face to face with the man who had stolen part of her soul on that single night in a London hotel. The man whom she had tried to convince herself she never wanted to meet ever again. But the man whom she knew, deep down in her heart, she most longed to see in the entire world.

Until he had appeared in Helikos in the form of the one man that she must never, ever, even dream of getting close to. The man who was totally forbidden to her, and had to stay that way for the rest of her life.

CHAPTER TEN

'I'M SORRY.'

Skye felt obliged to say it.

'I never meant you to feel used.'

The truth was that it was the last thing she had expected.

'But can't we forget about that night—put it behind us?'

'You know damn well that we can't!'

Theo's voice was rough and husky and his eyes burned like polished jet as they scoured her face.

'It's still there—between us. I can't forget about it—can you?'

Never in her life, Skye acknowledged, but she was going to have to try. There was no way she and her family could have a future if she didn't escape from the past.

'I have to,' she said with what she hoped sounded like conviction. 'We have to. Nothing can happen between us. I'm marrying your father. We have to live as if we'd never met before. As if we'd never...'

'And you can do that, can you?' Theo put in when her voice failed her, lacking the courage to complete the sentence. His tone was dark with cynical scepticism, making his disbelief all too plain. 'You can pretend that we were never lovers—that we have only ever been stepmother and stepson?'

No! No, I can't do it—I can't bear it! Skye's heart felt as if it were being ripped in two at just the thought. She didn't want to be Theo's stepmother. She didn't feel at all motherly towards him. She wanted...

But she couldn't have what she wanted. That was forbidden to her. She had to put even the dream of it out of her mind and learn, somehow, to live with what was real.

She found the strength to straighten her back, lift her head. She even managed to look him straight in the face, meeting the black-ice stare of those coldly assessing eyes.

'Yes,' she managed, and was stunned to hear an assurance that she could never have felt actually sounding in her voice.

But was it enough to convince Theo? He *had* to be convinced. She didn't know how she could go on if he wasn't.

He didn't look convinced. But then she didn't know what he *did* look. She couldn't read his still, inscrutable expression. Couldn't tell a single thought that was passing through his coolly assessing brain. She could only hope and pray.

Still with his eyes fixed on her face, Theo stirred slightly. He drew in a long, thoughtful breath, inclined his head to one side, ever so slightly.

'Prove it,' he said.

'What?'

'Prove it,' Theo repeated, with a harder, slashing emphasis. 'If you're so convinced that you can act as if we've never been lovers—as if there is nothing between us—then do it. And get some practice in before my father comes home. He said I would look after you; I think I'd better start doing that.'

'But...' Skye tried to protest, but Theo cut through her stumbling attempt to speak.

'Spend the rest of the day with me. We'll do a guided tour of the island—that seems like the sort of thing a good stepson would do. Be my stepmother—nothing more. And if at the end of the day you can still say you can live with things that way, then I swear I'll leave you alone—for good.'

I'll leave you alone—for good.

Skye's mind swung violently between hope and despair;

agreement and total, desolate rejection of his suggestion. One part of her wanted to do this so that he would leave her in peace—and yet the thing she most wanted in all the world was that he would never leave her. But the way she wanted that was what was totally forbidden to her.

She was going to have to learn to live with that. And perhaps the way that Theo had suggested—the idea of practising, of trying to get used to the idea, without the fear of having Cyril's eyes following every move—might just work.

She didn't know. But the one thing she was sure of was that the ruthless, determined set of Theo's hard features made it only too plain that if she refused then he would put his own interpretation on that fact. An interpretation that spelt death to her hopes of any peace of mind in the future.

It seemed to her that she had only one possible choice.

'All right,' she said slowly. 'I'll do it.'

Was he really going through with this? Theo asked himself when they were in the car and heading down the rough, winding road that led away from the house. What had happened to his doubts, to the private acknowledgement of the risks he ran, the temptation he would have to endure if he stayed?

The truth was that he *wanted* that temptation. He couldn't turn away and just leave it. When he was with Skye he felt more involved with everything, more *alive* than ever before, and he wasn't going to abandon a chance to experience that sensation once more, even if it was for the last time.

Besides, he hadn't been back to Helikos in all the five years he had been apart from his father. He wanted to reacquaint himself with the place, revisit his favourite spots, the places he had loved as a boy. And he would enjoy seeing them afresh through her eyes.

'We'll follow the coast road first,' he told her. 'That way we can visit the ruined monastery and take a look at some of the caves before we head for the village. I know a wonderful little *taverna* where we can eat dinner. The people who own it were like family to me.'

And almost more than family, he recalled. Berenice, the oldest daughter, a woman not much more than five years older than himself, had had an intense affair with his father at about the time that the old man had tried to push his son into an unwanted marriage. He remembered how, in one of the last conversations he had had with Cyril, he had flung the fact into the older man's face.

'If you're so desperate to have more heirs,' he had shouted, 'then why don't you marry your mistress? Start a new family with her!'

'I might just do that!' Cyril had responded.

But it seemed that now Berenice was out of the picture. Obviously, his father had thought twice about making a simple village woman the fifth Mrs Antonakos.

Instead he had chosen this English girl who was less than half his age. A girl who was not at all the type his father usually went for.

Berenice was much more his father's type. Cyril Antonakos was drawn to that small, black-haired, dark-eyed, full-bosomed type of woman. Not the tall, slim, Titian-haired seductress that Skye Marston was.

A woman who, simply by existing, made Theo live in a state of constant hunger, of a desire so hot and painful that it was an agony of frustration to sit so close to her in the confined space of the car. An agony of yearning to inhale the delicate fragrance of her skin with every breath he took, and not do anything about it.

A woman who made him want to slam on the brakes,

bring the car to a screeching halt and turn in his seat, reaching out for her in desperation. Made him want to drag her into his arms, haul her close and take her mouth, kissing her hard and long, demandingly, until they were both senseless with heady desire, an explosive cocktail of hunger and frantic passion impossible to control.

'*Theos*...' Cursing under his breath, Theo gripped the steering wheel so tightly that the knuckles on his hands showed white under the tanned skin. Pebbles flew up from underneath the tyres, clanging against the underside of the car and making Skye look up in stunned confusion.

'Is there a problem?'

'I forgot how primitive the island roads can be. You can't afford to let your concentration slip for a moment.'

'The view has much the same effect,' she smiled. 'I never knew the sea could be so many wonderful shades of blue.'

If she smiled at him like that once more, then he was lost. Theo forced his attention back to the road

'This is October. You should see it in the summer—it's like the most brilliant jewel in all the world then.'

'I'd love to see it.'

Skye's voice had an odd little break in it, one that made it sound suddenly vulnerable and dangerously appealing so that Theo had to clench his jaw tight against the way that that softness twisted in his guts.

'You will do,' he said, the fight he was having with himself making his words come out far more harshly than he wanted. 'You'll be living here then—as my stepmama.'

If he had reached out and slapped her hard across the face, it couldn't have had a more dramatic effect on her. She shrank back inside herself like a small, frightened rabbit retreating into the protection of its burrow. The sudden clouding of her eyes and the way that her sharp white teeth dug into the softness of her mouth were like a reproach to him, making him curse himself for the roughness of his reply.

But at least she had lost that tempting smile. And the way that she turned from him, fixing her concentration back onto the azure spread of the ocean at the bottom of the dramatic fall of the cliffs, meant that temptation no longer tormented him with thoughts of the softness of her breasts beneath the lilac dress, the shortness of her skirt.

If she kept her back turned to him, her gaze on the view before her, then he might just be able to keep a grip on the hunger; stop it from running away with the last bit of sense he possessed.

If she kept her back turned to him, her gaze on the view before her, then she might just be able to keep a grip on her emotions, Skye told herself. She had made a near fatal mistake in turning, in smiling at him, as she had.

Turning had brought her too close to him. It had made her so intensely aware of his physical presence beside her. She had inhaled the scent of his body with her swiftly in-drawn breath, and her smile had been directed straight into those watchful black eyes. And she was sure there had been some flicker of response in them that had had her holding her breath in disbelief.

But then suddenly he had changed. She had seen it in his face, heard it in the tone of his voice as he had drawled cruelly, 'You'll be living here then—as my stepmama.'

Did he know how much it hurt to be slapped in the face by that reminder? He had to. It was why he had done it. He was making sure that she remembered exactly where she would stand with him if she went through with the marriage to his father.

A marriage she *had* to go through with if she was to have any chance of ensuring her parents' future.

And any chance of saving her mother's life. The memory of the phone call she had had with her father last night

invaded her head, dragging dark shadows with it. She had
wanted to speak to her mother, but Claire Marston had been
sleeping. They weren't prepared to wake her...

A tiny gasping sob escaped her, impossible to hold back.
She had been a fool to think that she could ever go through
with this stepmother act.

'What's wrong?'

The hard demand sliced through the atmosphere inside
the car like a slashing knife, making her jump with the
force of it.

'Nothing.'

Her heart lurched painfully as she heard his muttered
curse and felt the car come to an abrupt halt, spraying pebbles wildly around the tyres.

'Something has upset you and I want to know what.'

'Do you really have to ask?' Skye twisted in her seat,
turning back to face him, blinking ferociously to drive away
the weak and revealing tears in her eyes.

'I mean—I'm sure you know only too well. Or can
guess. Why are you so determined that I shouldn't marry
your father?' she demanded when she saw his dark frown
of incomprehension. 'Why does it matter so much to you?'

'Because you would be living a lie—we both would.'

'We had one night together! It doesn't have to affect the
rest of our lives.'

'One night I can't forget. And I don't believe you can
either.'

There was no hint of yielding in his face. His features
were set in hard, ruthless lines, his eyes glittering with the
coldest anger.

'You were a virgin—you know what they say about always remembering your first.'

That burned so much into her already wounded soul that
Skye closed her eyes briefly against the pain. But then she
immediately forced them open again, dragging herself back

into the role of careless indifference she had chosen for her own protection.

'Well, don't flatter yourself that that's true for me. You might want to imagine that you were unforgettable, but I'm afraid that's just not the case.'

Not true, her outraged conscience reproached her, crying out against the betrayal of the truth. She hadn't forgotten Theo's touch, his kisses, his lovemaking. The vivid intensity of her memories, the blazing Technicolor brilliance of her dreams, left her in no doubt at all that the images would never fade.

She'd insulted him savagely too. She could see it in the flaring rage in the black brilliance of his eyes, the tightness of every muscle in his face that scored white lines of fury around his nose and mouth, stretched the skin ferociously over the broad cheekbones. It hurt to see what she had done, and she longed to open her mouth and protest sharply, to take back the terrible words. But even as her conscience lashed at her for the lies, her sense of self-protection recognised the need for it; the shield she had put up against the dangers of letting this man get too close.

But he was already too close, she admitted miserably. He was in her mind all day, every day. In her dreams each night.

In her heart.

But *no*! She wouldn't allow herself to let that idea into her head. She couldn't risk it, didn't dare to even consider the possibility that she had come to care for Theo Antonakos more than was safe.

'Is that why you bolted? Because I was so *forgettable*?'

He was starting the car again as he spoke. Starting it with a roar and a crunch of gears that, even after such a short acquaintance with his driving techniques, she knew was completely non-typical of him.

He was beyond angry. He was furious—coldly furious.

But while she shivered inside at the thought of his rage, she also welcomed it. His loss of temper had distracted him, taken him away from the thought of probing into why she had been so upset. It had stopped him from asking any more questions that she would find impossible to answer and so, while she couldn't relax, she could at least feel that she only had one thing to concentrate on. Theo's obvious dislike of and contempt for the woman she was pretending to be, the mask she was hiding behind, was hard enough to cope with. But at least it kept him from digging any deeper into areas that she couldn't even begin to explain.

'Or was it that you were shocked rigid at the discovery of your own sensuality and you were running scared?'

'I wasn't scared! What is there to be scared of?'

'What?'

Once more the car screeched to a halt on the deserted road. Theo had barely had time to yank on the brake before he had flung off his seat belt and was turning towards her, grabbing hold of her arms and pulling her towards him with a force that made her own seat belt lock, holding her immobile.

Cursing savagely, he stabbed a long finger on the button that released the strap, catching her as she tumbled into his arms.

'What is there to be scared of? I'll show you...'

Arms like steels bands fastened around her, twisting her in her seat as he hauled her up against him. His mouth came down on hers with a savage demand, crushing her lips cruelly and forcing them open under the pressure of his.

But then, in the space of a single, jerking heartbeat, everything changed. Her mouth wasn't crushed open, but yielding swiftly and softly, letting him in rather than having no option. The taste of him was as intoxicating as fine wine, rushing straight to her head, coiling along her senses so that she couldn't get enough of him. Her tongue tangled with his, taking in more of him, inviting, offering more of herself. And he took it. He took her mouth, he took her senses, he took her hunger and fed it, making it grow and rage out of control.

His hands were moving over her body, stroking, caressing, tantalising. Never once demanding, and yet the yearning ache, the throbbing pulse that woke between her thighs created a stinging need that was a fiendish combination of the darkest pleasure and the sharpest pain. Her fingers were clawing at his chest, fastening over his shoulder, digging into hard, taut muscle under the smooth cotton of his shirt. But she couldn't keep them still. Sliding upwards, they tangled in his hair, twisting in the black silken strands, holding him prisoner, his mouth still on hers, when she feared he would move away.

She didn't want this to end. She couldn't bear it if it had to stop. She felt she would die, or at least some vital part of her would cease to exist. She wished she were anywhere but here, in the cramped discomfort of the luxurious car's front seat, where the brake handle and other controls poked into her side, her hips, prevented her from getting just as close as she most wanted.

She wanted to be somewhere where she could take this further—where he could take *her*. Where they could take each other. Her heated, frenzied fantasies were already forming images of forcing open the car door, and tumbling out onto the grass verge at the side of the road, dragging Theo with her, when, with a low, protesting moan, he wrenched himself free, pulling his mouth from hers and flinging himself back in his seat.

His chest was heaving raggedly, his breath snatched in, rough and raw. His head was thrown back, exposing the long, tanned line of his throat, his hair wildly tousled from the effects of her clutching hands, and his eyes were closed.

clamped tight as if he didn't *want* to see. Didn't want to face reality, but to concentrate instead on the blazing inner world that had sent flame searing through his senses, wild as the smallest spark through bone-dry tinder.

'*Theos!*'

The word was barely formed. It was just a gasping sound, forced from a throat that was raw and dry and as husky as if it pained him desperately to speak.

'You ask what there is to be afraid of! *That's* what! And if it doesn't scare you, then it sure as hell scares the life out of me! It makes me forget what I believe is right—the way I believe I should act...'

Skye didn't know if she was shaking with fear at his reaction or with the ferocity of the sensual response he had drawn from her. She was trembling like a leaf and yet at the same time she had never felt more alive in her whole life. Her whole body was in a state of stinging awareness, so much so that to have been pushed away from him as she had felt like a little death, a terrible loss that left her feeling bereft and desolated.

'*That's* why you can't marry my father—admit it, damn you!'

Skye couldn't say a word. Couldn't open her mouth or she would give herself away. Just her tone would reveal how devastated she was, how true his words were. He wouldn't even need to challenge her to admit it—her voice alone would betray her.

And so she kept silent. But so did Theo.

And there was something about his silence—some fierce, withdrawn, brutally controlled quality that twisted in her heart and added a whole new dimension to her despair.

She hadn't meant to entangle him in all this. Hadn't ever thought that he would become involved in her own private hell. And she didn't want to make him feel this way. The terrible sense of frustration and guilt and scorching, blazing need was bad enough when she was enduring it herself. The thought of having forced someone else to go through it—and to know that there was no way she could do anything about it—appalled her right to her soul.

'Theo…'

With a shaking hand she reached out to touch his thigh, only to have him snap upright, knocking her hand away from him with a rough, jerky movement.

'Don't!' he commanded in a voice that still carried the echoes of the sensual storm that had shaken them both. 'Don't ever touch me again! You see what happens when we touch! We both go up in flames! We're not safe to be together.'

Shadowed dark eyes slid sideways to study her face, the question she didn't want him to ask burning deep inside them.

'Not if you're determined to stick to this mad idea of marriage.'

How did she answer that? There was only one possible response she could give, even if her heart rebelled against it all the way.

'Are you still set on marrying my father?'

'If he'll have me.'

'Then stay the hell away from me.'

Theo didn't care if he was being unfair. He knew she would only have to say that she hadn't come anywhere near him—that he was the one who had pounced on *her*—and he wouldn't have a leg to stand on. But right now he wasn't feeling at all fair. He wasn't even feeling in the least bit in control.

The sensual storm that had exploded in his body had taken his mind with it. And he was still having to fight the raging need that turned his body to fire, made his blood run molten through his veins.

He didn't even dare to look at her straight. If he did he

would see her soft mouth swollen with his kisses, the glorious red-gold hair mussed and tangled, her jacket awry, skirt pulled up over her thighs. If he did, then the fires he was struggling to damp down in a body that was still hard and aching with need would flare up again in a second, and this time he might not be able to hold them back.

'I told you—we're not safe to be together.'

'Then you'd better turn this car right round and take me back.'

'I thought you wanted to see the island.'

'I did. But...'

Theo shook himself inwardly, trying to bring some sense to his whirling thoughts.

'I said I'd show you the island.' His voice was rigid with control. 'If we stay out in the open—stick to public places—we should be okay. It has to be a damn sight safer than going back to the villa.'

He wanted to show her Helikos, damn it! He wanted her to see his favourite places—the beach where he had run wild as a child, the ruined monastery where he had played games of imaginary knights and dragons, and where his mother and her family were buried. The village where he had made friends with a few, forbidden village boys and where later—in his adolescence—he had learned more about the opposite sex than his father ever suspected.

He wanted to see those places anew through her eyes. And, yes, if he told the truth, he wanted to be the one who showed them to her, not his father.

It was time he admitted the truth. He was jealous as hell of his own father. Jealous of the fact that the old man was engaged to this stunning woman—that she seemed determined to marry him, even if only for her own mercenary reasons. It might be weak, it might be foolish—it might be downright crassly stupid—but right now he reckoned he'd settle for being used for his money if it meant having Skye Marston in his bed once again.

Admit it, he told himself: he'd do anything—sell his soul if necessary—for that. But his only chance of convincing her that she didn't need to marry his father was to spend time with her. And if the constant ache in his groin and the raging nag of frustration was the cost of that time, then he'd pay that too. If it was that or nothing, then he wasn't going to settle for nothing.

'Just think of me as your private tour guide,' he managed to say with a reasonable degree of conviction. 'I'll be the soul of discretion. I promise.'

The look she shot him was sidelong and filled with disbelieving scepticism.

'You have my word,' Theo assured her. 'I'll behave just as I should when I'm out with my stepmother-to-be.'

He meant it too. Meant it all the more because of the way that her face changed when he said those last three words.

And the fact that she clearly hated being described as his future stepmother just as much as he hated describing her that way gave Theo such a personal satisfaction that he smiled secretly to himself as he put the car in motion again.

He'd behave like the perfect stepson, all right. He wouldn't put a foot wrong. And if the lovely Skye found that she didn't like being treated that way—well, that suited him down to the ground.

CHAPTER ELEVEN

THEO stuck to his word for almost all the afternoon. He was the perfect escort, and the perfect stepson. He was cool, polite, attentive, but not too attentive, considerate, helpful...and nothing more.

At least externally.

Inside his head it was a completely different matter.

No stepson should ever harbour the thoughts about his stepmother that he did. He certainly shouldn't notice the sway of her breasts under the soft cotton of her dress, or the way her legs tightened as she climbed the cliff walk to the ruined monastery. He shouldn't notice how slender and soft her feet were when she pulled off her shoes to walk barefoot over the sand and paddle her toes in the sea that lapped against the beach. And he most definitely shouldn't have wanted to swing her into his arms and kiss her senseless, carrying her away from the shore, to find a secret hidden place where he could strip the clothes from her body and make mad, passionate love to her until they were both too dazed even to think.

But those thoughts were the ones he kept hidden inside his mind. To Skye's face he was totally in control, driving her all around the island, telling her the history of the places they visited, and adding personal tales of his own childhood to entertain her. He taught her words of his language here and there and finally, as the shadows of the gathering dusk began to fall about them, he took her to the small *taverna* in the village where he introduced her to the best of the local food.

'This is wonderful!' Skye exclaimed, washing down the

last morsel of a tasty filo roll stuffed with spinach with a swallow of crisp white wine. 'What did you say it was called again?'

'*Bourekakia,*' Theo told her, smiling in response to her enthusiasm.

It was impossible not to smile when she looked at him like that, her eyes sparkling in the light from the candles that stood on every scrubbed wood table top. Her skin glowed after the afternoon spent in the open air, colour washed into her cheeks by the wind that had blown in from the sea. She had caught her hair back loosely, tying it with a turquoise silk scarf, and silver earrings gleamed on the lobes of her exposed ears.

'*Bourekakia.*' Skye struggled to get her tongue around the syllables. 'I must definitely have those again! They were delicious. And to think that until now the only thing I ever ate that was Greek was a feta salad.'

The earrings danced as she laughed. Earrings he had bought for her in one of the tiny shops in the village; little more than a single room where craftsmen worked to traditional designs handed down from father to son over a century or more. She had fallen in love with the tiny silver dolphins on sight and he hadn't been able to resist making an excuse to go back and buy them when she had been distracted by an array of belts at a leather goods stall.

It wasn't breaking his promise to stick to the rules, he told himself. He would have done the same for a prospective stepmother who was much closer to his father's age if she had expressed the same delight in the jewellery. The earrings wouldn't have looked as stunning on anyone else, though. The beautifully curved shaped of the dolphins' bodies accentuated the graceful lines of Skye's slender neck, and the polished silver gleamed softly against the glorious colour of her hair.

The temptation to reach out and touch the delicate silver,

using it as an excuse to stroke his fingers down the equally elegant length of her throat, was almost irresistible and he had to reach for his own glass in order to distract himself from the dangerous appeal.

'Oh, Iannis can make you a salad if you want. But I think that what you've ordered for your main course...'

His voice trailed off as he spotted a waitress bringing a bottle of wine to a nearby table.

'Berenice!'

The woman who had been his father's mistress.

'Excuse me.'

'Of course.'

What else could she say? Skye asked herself as Theo tossed down his napkin, pushing back his chair as he did so. *No? Of course I won't excuse you—not if you're going to speak to her!*

She had no right to say any such thing. No excuse for keeping him here at the table with her and nothing to explain the automatic protest that leapt to her lips and could only just be swallowed down in time before she opened her mouth and let it out, giving herself away in the process.

She didn't want him to leave her. Certainly not if he was going to speak to another woman—especially one as stunning and sensually feminine as this sloe-eyed, black-haired beauty who was smiling a warm and open welcome as Theo approached.

But the only justification for the feelings she had came tangled up in a word that she didn't want to let into her thoughts. A word that she knew was the one that described what she felt, but that she didn't want to acknowledge because the emotions behind it were too dangerous, too threatening, too overwhelmingly terrifying to be able to cope with right here and now.

That word was *jealousy*.

She was jealous of the woman whose appearance had

pulled Theo to his feet with such speed. She was jealous of the smile that had lit his face, sparking in his eyes as he had recognised her, said her name. And she was jealous of the answering smile on this Berenice's lips and the evident warmth of her greeting.

She was jealous.

She was more than just jealous. She was eaten up with the horrible feeling. Fighting to stay in her seat and not jump up and march over to where Theo and this Berenice were engaged in an animated conversation.

Leave him alone! He's mine!

'Oh, no!'

The words escaped in a shocked whisper and Skye reached for her wineglass, swallowing down a large mouthful as the shock of her thoughts rocked her sense of reality, triggering off a series of shivering explosions along her skin and down her spine, making her shudder in fearful response.

It couldn't have happened to her—could it?

But another swift glance across the room, meant to calm her, to convince her that nothing had happened, that her fears were only imaginary, had the exact opposite effect.

The first impact was physical. It was as if she were seeing him again with brand new eyes. Seeing the tall, powerful form, the straight shoulders, strong chest tapering down to a narrow waist and long, muscular legs. In the flickering light of the many candles that lit the *taverna,* his strongly carved features and deep-set black eyes looked like the face on one of the statues of the ancient gods of mythology. And the glossy black hair fell forward over his forehead as he bent towards Berenice, his attention fixed totally on her.

And it was that attention, the absolute concentration on her and what she was saying, that made Skye realise something else. Something much more shocking and disturbing to her mental balance.

She couldn't bear to see Theo with another woman. Couldn't bear to see this Berenice looking up into his face, big dark eyes locking with his as she spoke softly and rapidly in Greek.

The sudden sombreness of his expression, his total stillness, told her that the two of them were discussing something important, something they didn't want Skye to share, and that knowledge twisted sharply in her suddenly devastated heart. And when Theo leaned forward, kissing the other woman lightly on the cheek, she felt her eyes burn with tears. Tears that made the image before her blur and swim disturbingly, like an out-of-focus film.

Her hands went up to the lobes of her ears where the delicate silver earrings hung.

Theo had bought her those. She had adored them on sight but, always conscious of the need not to spend money she didn't have, had reluctantly left them where they were. She hadn't even been aware of the fact that Theo had noticed how much she had liked them until they had sat down at the table in this *taverna* and he had slid a small package across the table to her.

'A souvenir of your first visit to Helikos,' he'd said in a casual, almost throw-away tone.

Foolishly she'd taken the gift out of all proportion. She been so thrilled that she had worn the earrings right away, twisting and turning her wineglass to try and see the effect they had in her reflection, and all the while grinning like an excited child.

And all that Theo had said was, 'I'm glad you like them.'

The earrings might have been out of her price range, but to a man of Theo's wealth they were simply a cheap trinket, something he could have bought a thousand times over and not even missed the cost.

But to Skye they meant so much more.

And that 'more' now forced her to face exactly why she was feeling the way she was.

She was jealous because she had fallen in love. She had fallen head over heels in love with Theo Antonakos, the man she could never have, the man who was totally forbidden to her.

She loved the son of the man she had to marry.

'Oh, no!' she whispered to herself, mentally falling headlong into the deepest, darkest pit of despair. 'Oh, please, please—no!'

But Theo was heading back towards the table and she had to collect herself, hide the way she was feeling.

'Sorry about that.'

He offered the apology in an abstracted, unfocused tone, one that jarred on Skye's already over-sensitised mood.

'No problem,' she mumbled.

She couldn't look him in the face. How did you look at a man in the moment that you had realised you were in love with him? And how could she look at the man she loved and know that he was lost to her for ever because she was going to—had to—marry his father?

But even though her whole body was singing in newly heightened response to the potent physical presence of the man opposite, it was obvious that he didn't feel the same. Glancing up through her eyelashes, she could see that Theo's attention wasn't on her. He was frowning down into his glass, black brows drawn sharply together and one strong hand tapping restlessly on the table, beating out a tattoo of impatience and irritation that she could find no explanation for.

But of course it was because of Berenice. He had been pleased to see her, but something the Greek woman had said to him had changed his mood totally.

What was she to him? Just a friend? From his initial reaction she had seemed more than that.

Was it possible that Theo could be seeing someone else and still make a play for her as he had?

Of course he could!

Reaching for her glass again, she emptied it in one swift, unwise swallow, feeling the wine hit her senses almost instantly.

Had that moment in the car at the beginning of the afternoon told her nothing? Had she learned nothing from the way that Theo had reached for her, the ferocious sensuality of his kiss, the savage passion that had flared between them instantly?

'What is there to be scared of?' she had asked him.

And he had shown her.

He had taken her into his arms and he had kissed her cruelly, ruthlessly, with a kiss that had nothing of caring or tenderness in it, but only of the determination to exert power, to control. To show her just what there was between them—blinding sexual passion, and nothing else.

He might as well have branded her with his mark of possession, like a slave of long ago; it would have had the same effect. She wore that brand on her heart anyway, knowing that she was his, and could never be anything else. Theo could feel for another woman, because his physical hunger for Skye was unleavened with any degree of caring. But Skye herself could only love him and, because her heart was given entirely into his hands, she could never feel for anyone else.

'We're going home.'

Theo's voice, rough and harsh, dragged her from the misery of her thoughts, her startled grey eyes flying to his face, seeing the shadows in the spectacular eyes. Shadows that had nothing to do with the flickering light of the candle flames.

'But we haven't eaten—the main course…'

'Are you hungry?' he demanded brusquely.

'Well—no—not really.'

The truth was that every scrap of the appetite she had had at the beginning of the meal had gone. Her earlier enthusiasm for the food now seemed light years away, and her stomach heaved nauseously at even the thought of it.

'Then we're going home.'

It wasn't up for debate, his tone said. And the way he pushed back his chair, the legs making an ugly, scraping sound on the tiled floor, emphasised that. He had decided, and he expected her to do as he said. But she didn't feel strong enough to fight his autocratic assumption that she would jump when he said, 'Jump.' And the truth was that if she did, then her protests would soon be revealed as the lies they were when their meals were brought and she couldn't eat any of it.

So she reached for her jacket from the back of her own chair and got up too. Theo dropped money onto the table top without even counting it, and then he was striding towards the door.

Unlike the way he had behaved on their way in, he didn't take Skye's arm to escort her, neither did he look back to see if she was following him. Whatever Berenice had said, it had clearly angered him terribly, and Skye shivered inwardly at the thought of just what might happen, what sort of mood he might be in when they were alone and in the privacy of the car.

To her astonishment her fears were unfounded. The fact was that Theo said nothing at all as he drove the car at a speed that was positively terrifying all the way back to the villa.

Even there he didn't speak, but left the car, slamming its door behind him, and marched straight into the living room where he poured himself a glass of brandy and took a large swallow, clearly making up for the way he had stuck strictly to water over dinner.

'Okay—so you're in a bad mood.' Pushed beyond the need for caution by the painful knots in her stomach, Skye surveyed him from the safety of the doorway. 'So are you going to explain?'

'You don't know what you're asking,' Theo returned flatly.

'I'm asking for an explanation. I reckon you owe me one after suddenly abandoning me in the middle of our meal together and going to talk to some other woman!'

No, that was totally unwise. She sounded like an insecure and jealous girlfriend. She sounded exactly as she *felt*. But not as she had any right to be.

'And then dragging me away from my meal before I'd even had a chance to taste it—'

'You said you weren't hungry.'

'Well, of course I wasn't hungry—not then. Who could have any appetite when you were glaring at them like a storm cloud from across the table?'

'My apologies.' He made it sound like anything but an apology. 'But I didn't want to stay there.'

'Then I think you owe me at least a reason for all this!'

'I owe you nothing!' Theo snarled, splashing another measure of brandy into his glass. 'All I promised was a trip around my island.'

'I'm not talking about the tour of your precious island!'

Something was wrong there.

Some sudden reaction, a tiny movement that he couldn't quite control, revealed Theo's feelings when she knew he would rather have died than let them show. There was a new wariness in the glittering black eyes, a tautness about his mouth and jaw that revealed she had come close to hitting home.

'Your island…' Skye said slowly as a whole new set of thoughts filtered down into her bewildered mind.

'My island,' Theo echoed darkly, watching her through narrowed eyes. 'What about my island, sweet Skye?'

It was his tone that convinced her. The cynically drawling way he spoke, the harsh emphasis on that 'my island'. It confirmed the way a suspicion had been eating away at her thoughts all the way through the trip around the island.

It was my mother's and it should have come to me. Theo's voice, dark with bitterness, rang inside her head from earlier that afternoon.

'Your father—he disinherited you.'

His only response was a hard, swift nod of his dark head, burning eyes still fixed on her face.

'Before your falling out, as his heir, you would have inherited Helikos. But now…'

'Now what, *agape mou*?' Theo prompted harshly when she hesitated, struggling with thoughts that stabbed at her like daggers. 'Just what is going through your fanciful little mind now?'

It was that 'fanciful' that pushed her into it. If he hadn't said that she might have chickened out, backtracking desperately and coming up with some other cover story to explain her reaction. But… 'fanciful' he had said, and the sardonic way the word had left his mouth, the cruelly mocking smile that had curved his sensual lips, incensed her, driving her over the top from cautious sense and into reckless determination.

'That's what's really behind all this, isn't it? Why you want to ruin things between your father and me. Why you want to make sure I never marry him. When your father disinherited you, you lost the chance to own this island at some time in the future. But as long as there was no one else, then there was always the chance that Cyril might change his mind…'

She was running out of steam, faltering in front of the steely-eyed glare that seemed to sear the skin from her face.

'Go on,' Theo prompted icily when she hesitated. 'I'm finding this all fascinating.'

'But—but if he married again, and had another child, then that child would become his heir in your place. You're determined to break up your father and me so that we don't marry—don't have children—and no one will come between you and your precious inheritance, Helikos.'

Catching her breath after the rush through the explanation, Skye fell silent and waited, her heart thumping cruelly, for Theo's reaction.

It was not what she expected.

He laughed. He actually threw back his head and laughed out loud. But it was not a kind laugh, not at all warm, and it definitely had no real humour in it. It was cold and cruel and deeply cynical, filled with dark mockery at her outburst.

'Oh, my dear Skye, if you really think that then you don't know me at all. If I was trying to stop my father from begetting another child, then I would be sorely disappointed. Because he already has a new heir—or he will have soon.'

'He can't! I mean—'

'Oh, I know that you told me that you and my father had never slept together. But one thing you should know, *agape mou*, is that my father has never, to my knowledge, ever been faithful to any one woman in his life. And he isn't starting now. He has a mistress. Her name is Berenice.'

He had put the glass down on the nearest table and Skye had the strangest idea that he had done so because he expected her to react in some way. But she couldn't. At least, not in the way that he was evidently expecting.

It was true it was a struggle to hold back on the feelings that were whirling inside her, pushing for expression, beat-

ing at her mind. But the emotions she was fighting not to
express were far from the ones that Theo was expecting.

Berenice was *Cyril's* lover. She had nothing to do with
Theo—except as his father's mistress!

Skye knew she was supposed to be shocked—perhaps
Theo even expected her to be upset, but inside her head
her thoughts were bubbling in wild relief and happiness.

'That woman in the *taverna*?' she managed, and her
voice was as shaky as Theo might have expected, if for
totally opposite reasons.

'The woman in the *taverna*,' he confirmed. 'She's been
my father's mistress for years—since before I left Helikos,
in fact. But she always feared she was barren—that she
couldn't have any children.'

'But now...' Skye supplied when he hesitated. Because
obviously there was a 'but' to come.

'Now she knows that's not the case,' Theo replied soberly. 'Berenice is three months pregnant and the child is
my father's.'

CHAPTER TWELVE

'YOUR father's?'

Skye had gone so white that Theo feared she might faint. In fact she was swaying weakly where she stood, as if her legs were about to give way beneath her.

'Skye?'

His voice was raw with concern. The truth was that he had never actually expected her to react like this. If he'd even suspected it, he would never have told her the truth quite so baldly and directly. But the way she had reacted to the fact that his father had a mistress had been so understated, almost as if she had been expecting it, that he had been more convinced than ever that she cared nothing for Cyril, and that she wouldn't care either to know about the baby that Berenice was expecting.

'Here—sit down.'

He moved to her side hastily, half leading, half carrying her to the settee and lowering her into it, coming down beside her on the soft cushions.

'I'm sorry—I shouldn't—'

''S all right,' Skye mumbled in a voice that made it blatantly plain it was not.

'No, it isn't. I—oh, hell, Skye!'

She had glanced at him as he spoke, looking up at him without the fall of her long auburn hair to hide her face. So he had seen the revealing sheen that glistened on her soft grey eyes.

'Tears?'

'No!'

She was stiffly defiant, her head coming up high and her smooth chin lifting determinedly.

But the mutinous expression and tone were completely ruined by the quaver in her voice. She had to struggle to control her mouth too, trying to clamp it into a hard line and failing abjectly. Somehow she had kept any tears from falling, but the wet drops had turned her long, lush lashes into damp, spiky clumps.

'Not tears!'

'Not tears?' Theo echoed softly. Lifting a finger to the corner of her eye, he brushed it against the softness of her lashes and brought it away wet. 'Then what are these?'

Skye's blurred gaze dropped to the hand he held out, focused on the moisture glistening on that finger. She stared at it as long, silent seconds ticked by, and he could almost feel the struggle she was having with herself not to reveal anything of what she was thinking.

But she couldn't hide the tiny, betraying signs. The way her throat worked as she swallowed. The small, undignified sniff.

And then a single tear fell onto his hand, hot and wet and desperately revealing.

'Oh, Skye!'

She muttered something, so low and thick with tears that he didn't catch it. But then she repeated it and this time there was no mistaking the desperation in the words.

'I can't...' Her voice broke on the word. 'I can't go through with this. I really can't!'

Theo couldn't put a name to the feelings that exploded inside him. Concern was there, and a powerful sense of sympathy for what she was going through. A need to understand—to know just what she meant—ran through everything like a seam of gold through the hardest rock. But there were other thoughts, less honourable ones, but ones he wouldn't have been human if he didn't admit to.

There was the sudden upsurge of triumph at the thought that he had finally got through to her—that he was finally seeing the real Skye after all. And surely tears meant that the real Skye was not quite as mercenary and corrupt as her declarations of why she had agreed to marry his father had made her appear.

But the one feeling he couldn't subdue was the way that he wanted—needed—her to say that what she couldn't go through with was the marriage to his father. For the first time he admitted to himself how much he had been waiting for just that moment.

'What?' he asked, still not moving, still not touching her.

He couldn't touch, not until he was sure. Because if he touched, then he would never, ever be able to let go again.

'What did you say?'

Her response came on a huge, gasping sigh. 'I can't…'

'You can't go through with this—with what? Skye, tell me—what can't you do?'

'I can't go through with this marriage!'

High and wild, the words were a wail of despair.

'I can't marry your father! I *won't*!'

And then, at last, the tears came with a vengeance. They welled up inside her eyes, drowning the shadowed grey, and turning it to glistening, blurring silver. The crystal drops spilled over, tumbled down her cheeks and dripped onto his hand, onto her dress, leaving dark, uneven splodges of moisture, soaking into the material.

But still she was totally silent. The tears streamed down her face, sheening her cheeks, dampening her hair, but she didn't make a sound.

And Theo found that that appalled him. Other women he had known had wept loudly, noisily, with great gasping sobs, and heaving breaths. Skye seemed like a marble statue, pale and still and totally silent.

Just the tears. The endless tears. And a terrible desolation in her eyes.

He couldn't hold back any longer.

'Come here!'

He enfolded her in his arms, hugged her to him. She buried her face in his shirt, resting her cheek on his chest. Her shoulders shook and the tears still came.

'Hush,' he soothed, stroking one hand down over the silky rope of her hair, feeling its springing softness beneath his fingers. 'Hush, *agape mou*…'

He found he was crooning to her in his own language, using soft words in Greek that he never would have said to her if he had thought that she might understand. In Greek he could call her sweet, and darling, he could tell her how beautiful he thought her, how he wanted to look after her, how he *wanted* her. Words that he could never use in her own language, to her face, because she would laugh, scorning them, and she would tell him that she had only wanted him for one night—nothing more.

And he had been right to think he must not touch her. From the moment that he had made contact with her slender body, he had known that he had stepped over the invisible line that was drawn between them. Between what was right and what was wrong. What they could and could not do. He had touched her and the feel of her softness, of the warmth of her skin, seemed to burn right up his fingers, searing along every nerve and setting it tingling as if from some wild electrical shock.

She seemed so small and fragile suddenly, the curve of her neck where her head rested against his chest so delicate and pale that it made his heart ache in longing. The scent of her skin and the sweet floral essence of her perfume coiled up around his senses, making his head swim with desire, tormenting him, driving him crazy with response. And the hard, cruel kick of sexual need that hardened his body, tightening sharply, was so primal a force that it almost made him groan aloud in yearning hunger.

She had stopped weeping now. The only way he knew it was that her shoulders had stopped shaking and she had seemed to freeze against him, totally still. But she wasn't moving away, and she kept her head pressed to his chest, her face hidden from view.

'Skye…' he said, stroking a hand down over her hair, tracing the line of fine bones at the point where her neck met her spine. Her name was almost indistinguishable in a voice that was thickened and rough with the arousal he could no longer hide.

She sighed and stirred faintly, but that was all. He sensed the warmth of her breath through the material of her shirt and it made his heart clench in sharp desire.

'Skye…'

This time her name was part sound, part caress against her skin as he kissed along the same path that his fingers had traced a moment before. His tongue touched her skin and he knew that nothing in the world had ever tasted so wonderful, so exceptional, unique. His fingers tugged at the silk scarf that fastened her hair, pulling it loose and letting it fall like a scented curtain all around them.

And then, in that secret world, he found he could ask. He could say the words.

'Did you mean that? When you said you couldn't marry my father?'

Under the burnished hair her head moved in a silent nod of acquiescence. His heart clenched cruelly, but that was not enough.

'Then say it! Say it, *agape mou*. Tell me *why*.'

'I can't marry your father because…'

It was so low that he might have missed it if he hadn't been straining to catch every tiny sound she made. But he caught it and the roar of his blood was like the sound of thunder inside his skull.

'Because it's you that I want.'

He needed no second urging. His dark head swept down, his mouth taking hers. They clung together, hands, bodies, lips, crushed so tight, so close that it seemed impossible to tell where the man ended and the woman began, her hair swirled around them, caught and clung to the roughness of his end-of-the-day stubble and held him prisoner like finest chains of silk.

Her mouth had opened under his, no hesitation, no restraint. But no yielding either. She was all need, fire and lightning and total abandon. And he couldn't wait any longer.

'Skye, my beautiful Skye, will you come to me now—come to my bed?'

'Yes,' she sighed against his lips, her body giving him the answer as she clung to him in need. 'Yes—please. But not here.'

Not here. He knew what she was saying. Not in his father's house.

Jackknifing to his feet, he scooped her up in his arms and lifted her from her seat. Carrying her with an ease that came from a sense of wild exultation, he shouldered his way out the door and into the shadowed darkness of the night. He carried her across the tiled courtyard where the water of the pool lapped against the sides, all colour drained from it in the moonlight.

The door to the pool house was left unlocked—no one ever came out this far into the countryside—and he kicked it open, marching in. Long strides made swift work of the short journey across the kitchen, the tiny living room, through another door.

And then they were in his bedroom where he lowered her to the bed and came down beside her, reaching for her, fingers twisting in the tangled hair, his hands cupping the fine bones of her skull as he brought his mouth down onto hers.

He had been afraid that the short trip from the house, the slight cooling touch of the night, might have dampened down some of the fire in her, lessening her ardour, but he need not have worried. If anything she met him with more enthusiasm than before, returned his kiss with a fervour that made his thoughts spin, and he threw himself down on top of her, crushing her underneath the hungry weight of his body.

Skye welcomed the heat and pressure that enclosed her. For a few heart-shaking seconds as Theo had carried her across the courtyard she had feared that the touch of the night air would cool his passion or hers, bring both of them to their senses with a rush. And whatever happened now, whatever the consequences, she didn't want to lose this wild delirium, the feeling of total right, total conviction.

She had no idea where this would lead. She didn't dare even to *think* of any such thing. All she knew was that she wanted this, wanted it more than anything else in her whole life, in her whole world. She didn't have any idea what would happen in the future—or if she even had a future—but right now she didn't care.

Knowing that no matter what happened she could never marry Cyril gave her a wild sort of freedom. She couldn't marry him, not if there was a baby to be considered, another woman who needed him, a child who needed a father.

What she would do about her family, her father's predicament, she didn't know. Somehow she would find a way. She would beg Cyril—do anything! But tonight she couldn't think about that. She couldn't think about anything but what she had right here and now. Tomorrow would have to take care of itself. She had tonight.

They had tonight.

It was nothing like that first time. Nothing like *that night* in London. There was none of the apprehension, none of the nervous worry.

She didn't feel any embarrassment at being almost naked with Theo, only wanted to touch and stroke and feel. She was tugging at his clothing before he had even dealt with hers, making him mutter in Greek in dark impatience when she stopped him from unfastening her bra because she wanted to rip his tee shirt off him, wanted the feel of his skin beneath her hands.

'Skye…'

The sound of her name was thick and sensual, a rough-edged, raw-toned mutter of impatient protest that made laughter bubble up inside her at the thought that she could reduce this big, powerful man to a state where he shook at her touch.

'Theo…' she returned, echoing both his accent and his intonation.

'Witch!'

He grabbed at her, turned her over until she was face down in the softness of the pillows. Holding her down with one hand, he wouldn't let her move until he had undone the strap of her bra one-handed, pulled it free and tossed it over his shoulder into the room. The sliver of white silk that was her only other covering proved trickier to remove single-handed, but he solved the problem by straddling her back and kissing his way down her spine. This created a sensation so erotically pleasurable that all she could do was lie still and submit, too given over to the delight of his touch to care that the last bit of her clothing was being eased down her legs as his kisses moved lower.

It was when she felt the heated pressure of his mouth on the softness of her buttocks that she moaned aloud in delight. His laughter was a warm sensation against her skin and he caught hold of her again, turned her back to face him.

'Now, you little temptress...'

But even as he laughed out the words, his mood changed dramatically.

Skye caught her breath in shock at the ferocity of the desire that blazed in his black eyes. His breath came harshly and a faint burn of red scored the line of his high cheekbones.

'You are beautiful.'

It was a sigh of pure sensuality and his hands had a faint tremor in them as he touched her face, traced the line of her cheeks. Those hard, knowing hands smoothed down either side of her neck, curved along her shoulders, then slid underneath her breasts to cup and hold their soft fullness, his thumbs stroking each pink, raised nipple in deliberate provocation.

'Oh, Theo...'

Sensation speared along every nerve, making her twist and arch under the pinioning weight of his body, and she saw his smile grow darker, deeper as he lowered himself onto her, his mouth taking hers in a hard, demanding kiss. Her need for him was a hot, heavy pulse between her thighs, the honeyed ache that this time she knew was only the beginning.

This time she recognised the start of sensations that could only grow—that would build and build until she was out of her mind with delight. And she wanted that. Wanted it so much that she pulled Theo down to her, taking all that his mouth could give while her impatient hands were busy with his belt, unfastening the button at his waist, sliding down his zip...

'*Agape mou*...' Theo choked as her seeking fingers found their goal, the heated hardness of him springing free of his clothing and into the welcoming embrace of her touch.

She curled her hands around the rigid shaft, instinctively stroking, teasing until he groaned in near desperate protest.

'You will spoil things for yourself, sweetheart,' he muttered against her ear. 'You're destroying my control.'

'And who said I wanted control?' she teased, letting her tongue trace the curving top of his ear, down the softness of its lobe. 'That's not what I'm looking for tonight.'

'Is that so? Then I think we are both looking for the same thing.'

He turned the removal of the last of his clothes into a sensual art, sliding his long body over hers as she eased away his jeans, his underwear. The powerful length of his legs came between hers, parting her thighs, opening her to him.

And at the same time his mouth tormented her sensitised and aching breasts. Hot hands lifted them towards him, his tongue coiling round and round each nipple in turn, bringing them to stinging, burning awareness, before taking first one and then the other into the warmth of his mouth, suckling softly, sending rivulets of fire running along the pathways of her nerves to pool in molten hunger at the core of her femininity.

'Theo!'

This time his name was an urgent reproach and she lifted her body to his, pushing herself against him, enticing, inviting, demanding.

A demand he had no hesitation in answering.

One fierce, wild thrust brought his body into hers, hard and sure. So hard, so sure that Skye flung back her head against the pillows and closed her eyes, concentrating all her being on the sensation of him filling her, being with her, taking her…

'*Ochi*—no!'

His sudden harsh protest stunned her, shocking her eyes

back open again. His hard face was directly above her, black eyes burning down into her startled grey ones.

'This time you do not close your eyes!' he told her roughly. 'This time you stay with me right to the very last moment. This time you *know* who is making love to you.'

Didn't he know? Couldn't he tell? Surely it was obvious that she couldn't be more aware of just whom she was with, who was making love to her? She had only ever given herself to one man like this. And she could only ever give herself in this way once in her life.

Tonight was the night that she made love with the man she loved. And if tonight was the only night she had left with him for the rest of her life, then no other night—no other man—would ever match it.

'I know who you are,' she tried, then lost the words in a moan of pleasure as he moved deep within her, pushing harder, further into her needy body. 'And I wouldn't want anyone else.'

'I'm glad to hear that.'

Theo's reply was a tiger's purr of triumph, rich and dark and husky with a blend of need and the deepest satisfaction.

'Because tonight I intend to spoil you for any other lover. After tonight you'll only be able to think of me.'

'I already do...'

Skye spoke fast to push away the bitter sting of that 'any other lover'. How could she know any other lover after this? How could she want any other man?

But then Theo moved again, his hand sliding intimately between their joined bodies, a knowing finger stroking her, exciting her with devastating effect. And at the same time his mouth closed over one erect nipple, faintly grazing it with his teeth, making her toss her head frantically on the pillow, her hair tangling wildly beneath her.

'Say my name,' he ordered thickly. 'Say my name.'

'Theo,' Skye responded in immediate obedience, incapable of any other reaction. 'Theo—Theo—*Theo!*'

Her voice rose almost to a scream on the last word, barely able to get the sound out. The combined assault upon her senses was driving her to the edge of distraction. She was so close that she could almost taste it…almost…

'Only me,' Theo muttered roughly against her yearning flesh. 'Only me.'

'Only you,' Skye echoed, not even knowing if her voice could be heard or not as she lost herself in the spiralling, whirling haze of need. 'Oh, yes—only…'

But the rest of her words were lost on a high, keening cry of fulfilment as she felt her senses soar and splinter into the final golden oblivion of ecstasy.

CHAPTER THIRTEEN

It WAS the phone that woke them late the next morning.

It was ringing in the main house, but there was an extension that was switched through to the pool house when there was no one at home, and the sound of it shrilling through the small apartment dragged them from the sleep of exhaustion.

Cursing softly, Theo padded through into the living room to answer it while Skye still struggled to wake properly, forcing her heavy lids to open reluctantly. But only moments later he was back, holding out the phone to her.

'For you,' he said flatly. 'From England. Your father.'

Skye didn't understand the look on his face, or the blank tone of his voice, but her need for news of her mother overrode all other thoughts so she almost grabbed at the phone, putting it hastily to her ear.

'Dad?'

Theo moved away into the other room—to give her privacy, Skye assumed. She heard the sound of the kettle being switched on, the clink of a spoon in a mug, but then something her father said forced her to concentrate hard.

It was ten minutes later that, having finished her call, switched off the phone and waited for Theo to come back, she realised that he was not in fact still being tactful. He was deliberately staying away and she had no idea why.

Throwing back the covers, she snatched at the nearest thing to hand that would cover her nakedness. It turned out to be the tee shirt Theo had been wearing last night, still bearing his imprint in the scent of his body that permeated the soft material. It was just long enough to reach to the tops of her thighs, exposing large amounts of slender leg. But there was no point in false modesty. Theo had seen— and touched, and *kissed*—every last inch of her throughout the night. There was little point in covering up now. Brushing her hands through her tangled hair in a vague attempt to restore it to some sort of order, she made her way into the living room.

Theo was standing by the open patio doors, staring out at the hazy mist that blurred the far horizon. He had pulled on a pair of jeans but nothing else, and she was shocked to see the way that the bronzed skin of his broad back still bore the marks of her nails where she had caught him in the throes of one particularly mind-blowing orgasm in the middle of the night.

'Theo?'

He didn't hear her, he was so absorbed in whatever occupied his thoughts. Padding silently on bare feet, she crossed the room unnoticed, lifting a soft hand to touch one of the small red weals.

'I'm sorry,' she said quietly. Then, 'Sorry!' more emphatically as he spun round in sudden shock.

Her tone changed abruptly as she saw his expression.

'Is something wrong?'

'I don't know.'

There was a worrying stiffness in his reply and the black eyes were opaque and distant. No longer those of the ardent lover of the night before.

'Why don't you tell me?'

'Tell you what? What do you want to know?'

Theo looked down at the still-full mug of coffee that was in his hand. Clearly he had made it and then forgotten to drink it, letting it grow cold as he became absorbed in whatever thoughts had preoccupied him out here while she was on the phone.

Grimacing in distaste, he tossed the unappetising liquid

out onto the stone paving beyond the window and dumped the empty mug on a nearby bookshelf.

'Why don't you start with why your parents aren't here?'

The mention of her parents made her tense instinctively. Even the tiny hairs at the back of her neck lifted in the instinctive reaction of a wary cat as she wondered if in fact he had been listening to her phone conversation after all.

With that phone call all the wild euphoria of the night before had evaporated like mist before the sun. Cold, hard reality had slammed home, rocking her world and sending her spinning into a yawning chasm of despair. All her fantasies of escape, of freedom, lay shattered at her feet, and her own foolish actions had made the situation so much worse. Now she had no idea which way to turn.

'If you are supposed to be marrying my father soon, then wouldn't your parents want to be at the wedding?'

That at least was easy to answer.

'My mother is ill—her heart. She's in hospital and too weak to travel.'

She tried to just make it a statement of fact, but the news she had just had from her father made that impossible. Her voice caught on the words, broke revealingly towards the end.

And Theo's keen hearing picked up on it straight away.

'It's bad?' he asked sharply.

This time Skye's voice deserted her and she could only nod silently as she struggled with the tears that burned in her throat, stung at the back of her eyes.

'How bad?'

'This operation that she's in for is her last hope.'

And now her foolishness of last night might just have destroyed all hope of the current treatment being successful. Last night, in a state of shock at the discovery of Cyril's mistress and her pregnancy, she'd thought only of the needs of that unborn child. This morning, with the news of her mother's condition far worse than she had anticipated, she had to consider her own family's needs. But there was no way that one could win out without destroying the hopes of the other.

'If it doesn't work then she'll—she'll need a transplant.'

'Then what the hell are you doing here? Why aren't you with her?'

'I wish I could be—but your father wanted me here.'

Sensing the next question, she rushed into answering it before Theo even had time to ask it.

'He wanted the marriage to take place as soon as possible...' Her voice trailed off, failing her once again as she saw the disbelief harden in his eyes, watched him shake his head in adamant rejection of her words.

'Surely even my father would wait. Skye—what is it that you're not telling me?'

Suddenly, ridiculously, Skye was desperately aware of her state of undress. The tee shirt that had seemed a reasonably adequate covering now seemed impossibly skimpy and revealing. Not at all the right sort of clothing in which to be having this sort of conversation.

But then, what sort of clothing *was* suitable for this sort of conversation?

Nervously she tugged at the hem of the shirt, painfully conscious of the fact that it did nothing to bring it any further down her thighs. All it did do was to draw Theo's black-eyed gaze to the point where her clothing ended and her legs began.

'There's something wrong here,' Theo went on, his tone making her shiver inside. 'And I want to know what it is.'

His face was set into lines of ruthless determination, telling her without words that there was no point in trying to appeal to his better nature—he just wasn't prepared to let this go.

Her heart felt as if it were breaking inside her. If he

pushed, she would have to answer. But she couldn't tell him the whole truth.

The truth that wasn't hers to tell.

And her father's phone call had just been a brutal reminder of how much that truth mattered. So she would have to go back to dealing in half-truths again. The terrible thing was that half-truths were also half-lies.

'Skye...'

The dangerous note in Theo's use of her name shocked her onto the defensive. She would have to go back to the cold, brittle role that had been her protection up to now.

'Th-there's nothing to tell.'

'No?'

If there was one thing Theo hated it was being lied to—and Skye was lying through her pretty teeth right now. He was convinced of that. Her beautiful eyes wouldn't quite meet his and she was shifting from one foot to another uneasily.

It would help him think more clearly if she weren't so distractingly dressed. He found it almost impossible to concentrate when she was standing there wearing nothing but the tee shirt he had discarded last night. The memory of the way she had stripped him of it, of the feel of her soft hands on his skin, on the most intimate parts of his body, made hot blood flood his veins so that he had to clamp down hard on the impulse to let his thoughts run riot.

'I don't believe you. And I want to find out just what's going on.'

'Nothing—' Skye began again, but Theo had had enough.

'All right!' he exploded, flinging out his hands in a gesture of wild exasperation. 'All right—so there's *nothing* there that you want to explain about. Well, we'll come back to that. Let's try a different tack instead.'

He'd caught her off balance there, that was obvious. Her

expression had changed, the defiant wariness in her eyes changing to a look of shocked confusion. She had even taken a step backwards, like a cornered animal.

'What—?' she began fearfully, but he didn't give her the chance to speak.

'There are other questions I want answering—questions you might find easier to answer, so we'll start with one of those, shall we? How about telling me about the night we first met?'

She was definitely on edge now. So much so that she was poised on the balls of her feet, looking as if she was about to run at any moment.

'What about that night?'

'You said that you agreed to marry my father because you wanted a wealthy husband.'

'I knew he could keep me in the manner to which I'd like to become accustomed.'

Skye's interjection sounded so unconcerned, so blasé, that for a moment he stopped dead, appalled by her carelessness. But then he looked into her eyes once more and saw the shadows that darkened their soft grey, the struggle she was having to meet his scrutiny, and he knew that he had to go on until he found out just what she was hiding.

'So, if that's the case, then why me? If you wanted a sugar-daddy for the rest of your life, why didn't you make sure of that before you went off the rails? Why the hell did you risk it all to sleep with me?'

Her chin came up higher, her eyes clashing with his in open defiance.

'You helped me—you came to my rescue. I was grateful.'

'Grateful!'

Theo echoed the word in bleak disgust.

'And so you slept with me! So tell me, my lovely Skye, is that how you plan to thank everyone, how you pay all your debts? Which makes me wonder—what the hell did my father do for you?'

She was backing away again, forcing him to move towards her if he was to keep this conversation going. All the colour had faded from her cheeks so that her hair was almost unbearably vivid, the deep pools of her eyes looking like bruises against the ashen white of her skin.

'I can't! It's none of your business!'

'I'm making it my business! Skye—tell me! What—?'

'Money!'

She flung the word into his face in a sort of wild despair. And then suddenly it was as if, having broken through some barrier, she could no longer hold anything back and the words just came pouring out.

'I told you—I needed money! There are debts—really bad debts. Debts I'll never meet on my own.'

'And my father said he'd pay them? But surely your parents…?'

'They have no more than I have! Less! And even if they could help me—do you think I'd ask? With my mother as ill as she is—it would kill her! So when your father offered marriage…'

'You snatched at his offer before he could change his mind.'

It had the dreadful ring of truth. And knowing his father, he could see that Cyril would not have been able to resist the macho prestige of being able to acquire a bride younger than his own son—even if he had to buy her to make it happen.

'It was my only way out. I couldn't see any other alternative. And he—he offered so much…'

'I'll bet he did. And so what was my part in all this?'

If it were possible, he would have sworn that she had gone even whiter. There wasn't a trace of blood left in her translucent skin.

'I—you—that was my last night of freedom. Your—Cyril was waiting for my answer. I had to give it to him the next day. I knew I was going to have to say yes—that from then on my life wouldn't be my own—and so I—I was looking for some...'

She seemed to struggle to find the right word, to get it out.

'Some fun.'

'*Fun!*'

The realisation that he had been nothing more than an act of rebellion against her upcoming marriage of convenience stuck in his throat, making him want to retch.

'That's all it was to you—some fun?'

'That's what it was supposed to be!'

There was an odd note in her voice. He was trying to get a handle on what it meant when she destroyed his concentration by adding, 'I hadn't reckoned on you turning up here afterwards.'

'I'll bet you didn't! And if I hadn't turned up, what would you have done? Lied?'

She actually flinched away from his words—or from the fury with which he flung them at her.

He felt furious. Furious with her for proving herself to have been as shallow and as grasping as he had feared she would be. And furious with himself because, even now, seeing her as she was, he still couldn't let go.

He had wanted that first night with her to prove to her that they could have more than the one-night stand that was all she had been prepared to offer him. Then he had wanted just one *more* night, to gorge himself on her, sate himself until he could walk away and not look back. Or that was what he had told himself.

But it hadn't worked out like that. Once again, a night with her had left him wanting, left him hungry. And like a fool he still wanted more. He couldn't let her go.

'You father asked for a bride. I would have been that bride.'

'Because he promised to pay off your debts? But you didn't expect the marriage to be any *fun*. Is that right? You could have played your cards better than that, sweetheart.'

'I don't know what you mean!'

'You had a better hand than you thought,' Theo elaborated cruelly. 'That night—when you chose me to have your *fun* with—if you'd been a little more clever, a little more wily, you could have found out more about me. You could have got yourself a husband who would give you more of what you wanted.'

Skye could hardly believe what she was hearing.

'A husband—are you saying that…?'

She couldn't frame the words. They just didn't seem possible.

'That if I'd known you needed a rich husband I would have applied for the job? That's exactly what I'm saying. I still am.'

No. Skye shook her head sharply. She couldn't have heard *that*. It was too much; too cruel.

'No?'

She heard Theo's mocking voice through a buzzing haze inside her head.

'Is that no, you didn't know—or no, you won't have me? Surely you're not going to turn down a husband who'll pay off your debts and not ask awkward questions about your virginity—and I think we've proved that we can provide that essential element of *fun* in bed.'

This couldn't be happening. Skye wanted to wrap her arms around her body to hold herself together. She was trembling in reaction and desperately wanted to hide the fact from him.

'Tempted?' Theo asked.

Tempted didn't describe it. It was all that she could ever have hoped for—all she had dreamed of since that night in London. She had dreamed that the man she had met and made love with—the man she had given her heart to—would somehow find her and come back into her life. That he would rescue her from the situation that had trapped her—tell her he loved her, and ask her to marry him.

Now it seemed that all her dreams had come true, but in the most bitterly ironic way possible. Theo was back in her life, he had asked her to marry him—but everything conspired to make sure that she couldn't say yes.

He didn't love her, for one thing. The most important, most essential thing. And even if she had felt she might be able to commit herself to a loveless marriage—as she had been prepared to endure with his father—it just wasn't possible. Theo might be able to pay off the debts her family owed, but there was so much more to the situation than just the money.

She had promised to marry Cyril in order to save her father from jail and if she didn't marry him then he would prosecute. That was the other reason why Andrew Marston had phoned her this morning. She could still hear his words ringing inside her head.

'You will go through with this, Skye, won't you? Promise me you will! I can't go to prison—it will kill me—and it will certainly kill your mother!'

A sound from outside caught her attention, bringing her head swinging round. The roar of a powerful car in the distance, coming up the road from the village.

Theo had heard it too.

'My father's back. When he finds you're not in the house, he'll come looking for you. It's decision time, *agape mou*. Which one is it to be—marriage to my father or to me?'

But Skye couldn't find any words to answer him. She was already dashing back to the bedroom, snatching up her

crumpled dress. It took only seconds to discard Theo's shirt
and pull on her clothes and by the time he appeared in the
doorway she was tugging down the lilac cotton and pushing
her feet into her shoes at the same time.

'I don't believe it!'

The contempt in his voice lashed at her and she winced
away from the brutal pain it brought to her already desolated heart.

'I have to do this,' she told him, grabbing a brush from
the top of a chest and dragging it roughly through her hair.
'Please understand!'

'Oh, I understand all right,' Theo declared, his tone harsh
enough to strip away a protective layer of skin. 'But you'd
better understand one thing too. I will wait one minute for
you to change your mind—and, if you do, then we'll go to
my father together. I'll tell him what happened—say I seduced you.'

'You'd do that for me?'

In a morning of shocks, this was the most unbelievable.
The last thing she would ever have thought she would hear
him say.

'But if you walk out of that door without me, then you
walk out for good. You never come back—is that understood?'

Skye nodded miserably. She could be in no doubt that
Theo meant the threat. She could also be in no doubt that
she was going to have to make him carry it out. She
couldn't tell him the truth and because of that she could
never do anything but leave.

'I'm sorry,' was all she could manage as she turned to
go.

For one appalling moment she thought that he was not
going to move, that he would not let her past. His strong
arm barred the way, one hand resting on the opposite side
of the door frame, blocking her path. Her heart slowed al-

most to a stop as burning black eyes clashed with troubled grey, Theo seeming to search for something in her face. She didn't know what he found there, but at last he lowered his arm to his side and stood back.

'You don't come back,' he repeated emphatically.

Knowing there was nothing she could say, Skye slipped past him and headed towards the door. Theo simply watched her go, arms folded across his chest and his face set like stone.

Tears blurred her eyes, almost blinding her as she stumbled her way across the courtyard, down the stone steps at the side of the house and into her room on the lower level.

She had barely closed the door behind her when Cyril's big car turned in at the gates.

CHAPTER FOURTEEN

SKYE put the last of her clothes into the suitcase and closed the lid. That was the final job done; there was nothing left to keep her there.

A long, desolate sigh escaped her. It was all she was capable of. No more tears. She was all cried out. At least for now.

She had no doubt that when she got home there would be more tears, more distress. She would have to try to explain things to her father, and she would have to take care of her mother. She didn't know how she would do it. She only knew she had to.

She had tried so hard to find a way out of this, but she knew that there wasn't one. Only the way that Cyril had offered and that was the one thing she knew she couldn't do.

Anything else she might have considered. But not that.

The car that Cyril had promised would take her to the helicopter was waiting at the door, a uniformed chauffeur standing beside it, cap pulled down low over his eyes. He took her case, saw her into the back seat, and closed the door, all without a word. Which was exactly the way she wanted it.

The truth was that she was barely conscious of her surroundings, of anything. She didn't have a word to say to anyone. The only man she wanted to speak to was determinedly absent, locked into the pool house, and she hadn't seen a sign of him since he had offered that dreadful ultimatum and watched her walk out.

And now she would never see him again. Ever.

The trip from the house to the helicopter pad was only a matter of minutes in the powerful car, and too soon, well before she was emotionally ready, they swung round the last bend and their destination came into sight. Clenching her hands tight over the handles of her bag, Skye forced herself to straighten in her seat, and prepare for their arrival.

Only to gasp in shock as the chauffeur brought the car to a smooth halt, still some distance away from the official parking place.

'What's the matter?'

The long hours of strain showed in her voice, making it raw and husky.

'Is something wrong? Do I have to walk from here?'

'No, that won't be necessary,' was the reply in a voice that made her heart stop violently in her chest, then launch back into action at double-quick time. 'I'll take you right to the launch pad if you like—and if you decide you want to go.'

Skye was too stunned to speak. Her tongue wouldn't work, her heart was now racing high up in her throat and her breath was snatched in raw, uneven gasps.

'*You?*' was all she managed to croak.

It didn't seem possible—it couldn't be true. But even as she forced out the question the man in the driving seat pulled off his cap and tossed it aside as he swivelled round to face her.

'*Kalimera,* Skye,' Theo said calmly.

'Wh-what are you doing here?'

It was hopelessly inane, but inanity was all she was capable of.

'I came to see you.'

'But you said that if I walked out—'

'I know.' Theo's voice was low. 'And I was a total fool to do so.'

He'd known he was a fool even as he'd been saying the

words. Known that the only, inevitable result of throwing out such an ultimatum was that it would blow up right in his face, leaving him with his life turned upside down and everything working out in the opposite way to what he wanted.

He wanted Skye to stay—there, he'd admitted it to himself once and for all. He wanted her to stay, and the last thing he needed was for her to walk away from him and never come back.

So what had he done?

Like a fool, he'd made it impossible for her to do anything else. He'd created a situation in which she was going to have to walk away because she had no choice. Hurt and angry, he'd pushed her into a corner from which she'd only had one possible escape route and then he'd been even more hurt and angry that she'd taken it. And he'd had to watch her walk away and known that he'd set up the whole situation in the first place.

The sense of loss—a real, tearing pain, far worse than the hurt pride that had pushed him into this—had wanted him to call her back. But anger, black, destructive anger, had kept him silent as he'd watched her walk away.

And when she'd gone he'd snatched up the coffee mug from the shelf where he'd placed it and hurled it against the wall, cursing savagely as he'd watched it splinter into a thousand tiny pieces.

'I put you in an impossible situation and then hated you when you reacted against it.'

'I had to talk to your father.' Skye's voice was very low.

'I know that now. I knew it as soon as I calmed down. But at the time I was just too damn blind to see. What can I say?'

He spread his hands in a gesture of resigned defeat.

'I was jealous. Jealousy does weird things to your mind.'

He'd shocked her there. She was sitting back in her seat,

wide grey eyes huge in a pale face. Wide grey, *red-rimmed* eyes. He hated himself for that evidence of tears just as he welcomed it as a sign of hope.

'Jealous?' she questioned now, a definite hesitancy on the word. 'Of who?'

'Of my father.'

Since she'd sat back, he couldn't see her properly, so he unclasped the seat belt quickly, freeing himself to turn enough to face her full on. He had to see her face. To know what she was feeling, if not what she was thinking. At least that way he might have some clue as to how to handle this.

'Hell, I reckon I've been jealous of every man in the world since I met you. But most of all my father.'

That was better. There had been a genuine flash of delight across her face when he'd said that. But it had been there and gone too quickly, too carefully masked for his liking.

'Why?'

'Isn't it obvious? Because I wanted you so much.'

It was more than that. Much more. He'd known how much from the way it had felt to watch her walk away and out of his life. But he wasn't ready to admit that yet.

'You made that clear.'

At least there was a flare of life in what she said. But was that life amusement or cynicism? The truth was that her tone was a mixture of both.

'Theo—the pilot is waiting.'

Was she so anxious to be gone? The thought rocked him, making him realise how much he was still taking for granted. He knew what he felt, but he had no idea what was going through *her* mind at all.

'No, he isn't,' he growled. 'Because there isn't a pilot.'

'Then how am I going to get off the island?'

'I'll fly you myself. If you have to go.'

'Of course I have to go! You know that I can't stay! Your father—'

'My father told me he'd ordered the pilot to get the helicopter ready, but I cancelled it.'

'You spoke to your father?'

'Of course I did. How do you think I knew when you were leaving?'

Skye felt as if the car must be rocking from side to side with the force of her emotions, first up and then down, until she no longer knew just where she was.

If he had spoken to his father, then she knew why he was here.

Cyril must have offered him the same sort of deal that he had offered her. A deal she had had to refuse. For the second time that day she had been offered a chance to have what she most wanted, most dreamed of in life, but under conditions that meant she had no alternative but to turn it down. Surely fate wouldn't be so cruel as to make her have to go through that again. Not when she was already having to endure this meeting as well.

Having resigned herself so unhappily to the fact that she was never going to see Theo again and then nerved herself for the journey home, it had been a stunning shock to find both resolutions overturned in a matter of seconds. It was too cruel of Theo—or fate, or whoever had decided it—to give her this one last look at his beloved face and know that she was going to have to leave him. Having said goodbye to him in her heart had been torment enough. But having to go through it all over again in reality was more than she could bear.

'Theo, please let me go! If you don't want me...'

'Damn it, woman! Weren't you listening? I just said that I wanted you—too much!'

'I know you did,' Skye admitted. 'But I think that what

you mean by *want* and what I mean are two very different things.'

In the seat in front, Theo stirred restlessly, one hand clenching into a fist and slamming down onto the leather covered back.

'Are you trying to deny that you wanted me every bit as much? Because if you are, then I don't believe—'

'No,' Skye cut in sadly. 'No, of course I'm not going to deny that. I'd be a fool to even try.'

'Then you do still want me?'

'Want?'

It was a shaken laugh and just for a second she leaned forward in her seat, acting on a foolish impulse to reach out and touch him. His face was just within reach, the lean line of his jaw faintly shadowed with dark stubble even at this time of the morning…

But she was forgetting about her seat belt, which snapped into place to hold her back, and she collapsed down in her seat again, letting out a sigh that was a blend of deep regret and a double-edged relief.

Regret because she longed to let her fingers rest on his dear face, to feel the satin warmth of his skin just once more, and relief because deep down inside she knew that if she *had* made contact, it wouldn't have stopped at that. There was no way she could have touched him and then done nothing more.

'Oh, yes, I want you,' she breathed. 'But if you've spoken to your father, then you know it won't work.'

In the darkness at the back of her thoughts, she could hear Cyril's words when she had finally got to see him earlier. She had decided to tell him everything—about her meeting with Theo that first time and what had happened ever since. She had been prepared to beg, to plead with him to help her father even if he wouldn't marry her. She'd offer to be his servant, nursemaid to the baby Berenice was expecting—anything.

She hadn't been able to say a word.

Cyril already knew about the baby, it seemed. That was why he had been so distant over the past few days; why he had gone to Athens to talk to his lawyer.

He had only planned to marry her in order to father a child. He had a child now and he was going to marry its mother, Berenice. So the arranged marriage between them would now not take place.

He was quite calm, totally businesslike about it.

But he had a proposition to put to Skye. One that would solve her problems—and those of her family.

'I've seen the way my son looks at you,' he said. 'He has a gleam in his eyes that gives away what he's thinking. He wants you, any man can see that. If you marry him, then our deal still stands…'

'Why didn't you tell me?'

Theo's voice interrupted her unhappy reflections, dragging her back to the present. He was leaning even further over the seat, black eyes burning into her face, and his voice was huskily intent.

'Why didn't you tell me about your father's problems?'

'They weren't mine to tell! I promised Dad I'd—'

She broke off sharply as he muttered something dark and dangerous in his native Greek.

'What did you say?'

Theo obviously made an effort to pull his black mood under control.

'I said that your father does not deserve your loyalty. What sort of man is he to let you go through this for his sake?'

'I said I would! And I was doing it for Mum as well. If my father goes to prison then it will kill her. She needs him so badly…'

Emotion forced her to stop, gulping down the tears that were welling up inside before she felt strong enough to go on.

'And Dad—Dad adores her so much that he would rather that I was unhappy than that he should lose her. He wouldn't want to live.'

'Now that I can understand,' Theo murmured, but Skye noticed that he did not loosen the strong hands that had clenched into tight, dangerous-looking fists on the back of the car seat. 'But I still cannot forgive.'

Forgive.

It was the last word that she expected and it drew her eyes to his face again. Looking more closely, looking beyond the grim set of his mouth, the tight muscles in his jaw, she saw unexpected shadows in the once brilliant dark eyes. It was as if, once the anger he had shown earlier had receded, it had left some sort of emotional bruising behind, marking his face with it. Just seeing that made her feel that perhaps she might dare open up to him a little more.

After all, what harm could it do? She and her family had nothing left to lose.

'Your father couldn't forgive either,' she said sadly. 'I don't know how I'm going to be able to tell Dad that—and Mum…'

This time she had to dig her teeth down hard into her bottom lip to hold back the tears and her eyes blurred so much that she didn't see Theo move.

'Don't!' he said sharply, suddenly leaning over the back of the seat and reaching out to stroke a soft thumb over the damaged lip. 'Don't do that.'

His tone took her breath away, froze her in her seat. Shock cleared her gaze so that she found herself looking into dark, deep eyes. Eyes that no longer seemed as hard as polished jet, but melting and liquid.

She was dreaming. She had to be. There was no way she

could trust her own vision. She was seeing things—or at least putting the interpretation she wanted on things that were really not that way.

'I'm forgetting…'

The soothing hand was snatched away so quickly that Skye almost moaned aloud, her own fingers coming up to cover the spot where his touch had rested. Under cover of their concealment, she savoured the taste of his skin on her mouth, then blinked hard in stunned amazement as Theo pulled a long white envelope from his pocket and tossed it onto the seat beside her.

'What's this?'

'Open it and see.'

It was the fact that he so clearly tried for nonchalance and failed that set her nerves jangling. Unfastening the uncomfortably restraining seat belt, she picked up the envelope and thumbed it open.

Inside was a single thick sheet of paper, printed on one side, with several signatures at the bottom. Disturbingly conscious of Theo's jet eyes on her, Skye skimmed through it hastily, then paused, frowning in shock, and went back to read it again.

It still didn't make any sense.

'I don't understand! This seems to say that your father isn't going to inform the police.'

'That's exactly what it does say.'

'But why? And what does this mean? This bit about "all accounts having been repaid…"'

'It means that your father's debts have been cleared.'

'By whom?'

She saw the answer in his eyes.

'Oh, no! Please don't say that you—'

'Of course, me.'

Theo couldn't believe her reaction. She actually looked

horrified at what he had done. When all the time he had been expecting—dreaming—planning…

If she truly was appalled, then where did that leave his next move? Unable to stay still in the confined space of the car any longer, he flung open the door and swung himself out into the crisp morning air. With a rough movement he pulled open the door to where she sat and leaned down to come face to face with her.

'Just what is wrong with that? Why the hell shouldn't I pay off your father's debts? And why shouldn't *my* father agree not to press charges? You don't really think that he would want to see my wife's father in jail for—'

'Your what?' Skye inserted in sharp question.

'My father-in-law,' Theo returned. 'Isn't it obvious my father wouldn't—?'

His words failed him when he saw the blank bewilderment on her face. Bewilderment mixed with total rejection of what he had just said.

'Don't you think you should ask me first?' she said in a tone so stiff that he half expected to be slapped in the face by the words as they came out.

It didn't surprise him, though. He'd blundered in, messing things up. He had to do this properly.

'I'm sorry—I rushed in—I was coming to that. I—'

There was only one thing for it. He was lowering himself to one knee outside the car, taking her hand in his.

'Skye. Will you—?'

But the look on her face was even more appalled than before. She snatched her hand back, cradling it to her as if it were burned.

'No—don't!' she gasped. 'Just don't! Don't do this—anything but this! Please, if you want payment, I'll pay you back if it takes my lifetime—but don't pretend you want to marry me! Please don't!'

If she had punched him hard in the face, Theo couldn't

have reeled back any more violently. He almost fell, but struggled to keep his balance and then got to his feet. Because he still held onto her hand, Skye had to go with him, scrambling awkwardly out of her seat and coming to stand beside him, facing him over the open car door.

'Just what—?' he began, but then broke off sharply.

What sort of an idiot was he? What did it take to get it through his thick skull? She didn't want to marry him; that was obvious. The best thing he could hope for now was to get out with some pride intact.

'I'm sorry,' he said, letting go of her hand and stepping back. 'I must have read the signals all wrong. I'm sorry.'

Skye's head was spinning. She didn't know what to believe.

Theo's proposal, his arrogant assumption that she would just fall in with his plans because they made her father his father-in-law, had been more than she could bear. Did he think that she didn't know *why* he was doing it? That his father hadn't talked of his plans with her?

And yet there had been that moment before he had let her hand drop when just for a moment he had closed his eyes as if to blot out the scene before him. And in that moment she had seen the flash of something very deep and very dark in his eyes.

In someone else she would have called it pain—but in Theo?

'I'm sorry too,' she said, stumbling over the words as she tried to get them out. 'I wish I could—you've been so kind…'

'*Kind?*' Theo echoed in a tone so savage it made her flinch from it. But she couldn't let herself be stopped now. She had to say this.

'I know that you think this way you'll get everything you want, and I'm sorry about the island, but—'

'Just a second,' Theo cut in. 'What the hell do you mean I'll get everything I want?'

'What your father promised. If you married me, you'd get your inheritance—get Helikos. I wish I could have done that for you. But I know how you felt when your father tried to force you into marriage before. If you married me, in time you'd regret it and—'

The expression on his face got through to her. He couldn't fake that look of blank confusion.

'You don't know what I'm talking about, do you?'

Theo shook his dark head slowly.

'Not an idea.'

'Your father never said that—that—if you married me he'd give you your inheritance—the island?'

'He'd have a problem—I already refused to have anything from him.'

Skye barely heard Theo's response, she was so determined to tell him everything.

'I knew how you hated it that first time when he wanted to tell you who to marry. I couldn't put you through that again. And I—I couldn't face the prospect that if you went into an arranged marriage with me then one day you might regret it so badly...'

'You're right. I would,' Theo inserted soberly.

'I thought s-so.'

It was a struggle to speak. The pain was so bad that it was tearing her apart inside.

But Theo hadn't finished.

'If I married you because my father dictated it and for no other reason, then, yes, I would regret it. Because that first time he tried, there was one thing it taught me—and that was I was so opposed to an arranged marriage because I only ever wanted to marry someone I loved. Someone I could share the rest of my life with. Someone I could grow old with.'

'I—I hope you find her.' It took all her strength to say it.

'I already have,' Theo responded softly.

He sounded totally strong, totally sure. She was falling apart. But then she saw the way he was looking at her.

'Who?' she had to ask.

'You,' he replied simply.

She couldn't have heard right. Her foolish, weak mind must have put the thought into her head. It couldn't be true! And yet…

'You—you said you'd already refused to have anything from your father?'

'That's right. As soon as I realised he was going to try to use Helikos as a bargaining tool, I knew I wanted nothing to do with it. If you thought that I was asking you to marry me because of what I would get out of it, then how would you ever know I adore you? And I do love you, Skye. I love you more than all the world.'

It was too much, too huge, too wonderful to take in.

'But you—I've seen how you love Helikos.'

'I love you more. And if I gained the island and lost you, then I would have lost the world. An island won't love me back, but I hope—pray—that one day you might find it in your heart to love me.'

'I already do.' Skye couldn't hold the words back any longer. 'I—'

But she got no further as Theo swept her up into a wild embrace, bringing his mouth down hard on hers in a kiss like no other they had ever shared. And as the world spun out of focus and into a golden haze of delight, Skye recognised just why it felt this way.

It was a kiss that was every bit as ardent and passionate and demanding as so many others they had shared. But this time, it was also a kiss of love.

When he finally released her, her eyes were sparkling

with tears. But they were tears of joy, of pure delight, of sheer, unadulterated happiness. Theo hugged her close, one hand coming softly under her chin to turn her face up to his, and his burning black eyes looked down into her glowing grey ones.

'So will you marry me, my love? Marry me and stay with me for the rest of my life so that I can spend my days showing you how much I care?'

Too full of joy to speak, she could only nod her heartfelt response, knowing that the way she was feeling couldn't be put into words, but showed in her face. And, just to make sure, she put her feelings into another long, glorious kiss.

'Tell me something,' she whispered when they finally found the strength to move apart—just a little. 'If I'd insisted on leaving, would you really have flown me away from here?'

'If I had to. But wherever you went, I would have gone too. I would never have let you out of my sight until I persuaded you to believe in my love for you—and to marry me.'

'Really?'

'Let me show you.'

Taking her hand, he led her to the back of the car and opened the boot. There beside her luggage was his case too.

'I'm packed and ready to go, my love,' Theo told her. 'I told my father I didn't want anything from him—except that pardon for your father. That's his wedding present to us and all I'll ever want from him. If I have you then I could never want for more.'

Reaching into the car, he pulled out the cases, then led her towards where the helicopter stood. And only now did she realise that the aircraft carried Theo's insignia on the side, not that of his father's corporation.

With the cases safely stowed, he turned to her once more and held out his hand.

'So, Skye, my love, will you come with me now? Come with me and start a new life—our married life?'

'It's what I want most in all the world,' she assured him.

A few moments later the engine roared, the blades spun and they took off from the island and headed into the bright light of their future. Together.

1205/01b

Modern
romance™

A RUTHLESS AGREEMENT by Helen Brooks

Lawyer Zeke Russell *always* wins. So when his ex-fiancée
Melody Taylor asks for help, he takes the chance to settle
an old score! Melody has no choice but to swallow
her pride and accept his proposition: rekindle their
relationship – though this time it's on *his* terms…

THE CARIDES PREGNANCY by Kim Lawrence

Naïve Becca Summer doesn't set out to be seduced by
Greek tycoon Christos Carides – but, with no love lost
between their families, he conceals his identity and she
falls into his bed! She longs to forget the bittersweet
memories of their lovemaking, but she's expecting
Christos's child…

PRINCE'S LOVE-CHILD by Carole Mortimer

Five years ago Sapphie Benedict lost her virginity to hunky
Hollywood screenwriter Rik Prince. But, thinking he
was in love with her sister, she left and didn't tell him of
the consequence of their affair! Now Sapphie meets Rik
again, and realises she has never stopped loving him. But
their lives are more complicated than ever…

MISTRESS ON DEMAND by Maggie Cox

Rich and irresistible, Dominic van Straten lived in a
different world from Sophie's. Even after their reckless,
hot encounter, she felt it best to go back to her ordinary
life. But Dominic wasn't about to let her go – he wanted
her as his full-time social hostess, travel partner and live-
in lover…

On sale 6th January 2006

*Available at most branches of WHSmith, Tesco, ASDA,
Borders, Eason, Sainsbury's and most bookshops*

Visit www.millsandboon.co.uk

FREE!

4 Books
and a surprise gift!

We would like to take this opportunity to thank you for reading this Mills & Boon® book by offering you the chance to take FOUR more specially selected titles from the Modern Romance™ series absolutely FREE! We're also making this offer to introduce you to the benefits of the Reader Service™—

- ★ **FREE home delivery**
- ★ **FREE gifts and competitions**
- ★ **FREE monthly Newsletter**
- ★ **Exclusive Reader Service offers**
- ★ **Books available before they're in the shops**

Accepting these FREE books and gift places you under no obligation to buy. you may cancel at any time. even after receiving your free shipment. Simply complete your details below and return the entire page to the address below. You don't even need a stamp!

YES! Please send me 4 free Modern Romance books and a surprise gift. I understand that unless you hear from me. I will receive 6 superb new titles every month for just £2.75 each. postage and packing free. I am under no obligation to purchase any books and may cancel my subscription at any time. The free books and gift will be mine to keep in any case.

P5ZEF

Ms/Mrs/Miss/Mr ....Initials ....

Surname .... **BLOCK CAPITALS PLEASE**

Address ....

....

....Postcode ....

Send this whole page to:
UK: FREEPOST CN81, Croydon, CR9 3WZ